HOPE BEYOND MEASURE

HOPE BEYOND MEASURE

By James Lacy

Published by
MIDNIGHT EXPRESS BOOKS

Hope Beyond Measure

Disclaimer

This novel is based on true events. Any references to real people, events, establishments, or locales are intended only to give the novel a sense of reality and authenticity. Other names, characters, and incidents occurring in the work are either the product of the author's imagination or are used fictitiously, as those fictionalized events and incidents involve real persons. Any character that happens to share the same name of a person who is an acquaintance of the author, past or present, is purely coincidental and is in no way intended to be an actual account involving that person.

Published by
MIDNIGHT EXPRESS BOOKS
POBox 69
Berryville AR 72616
(870) 210-3772
MEBooks1@yahoo.com

HOPE BEYOND MEASURE

By James Lacy

For mom, who never gave up on me; your patience and understanding will always be appreciated.

In memory of

Billy Smith, Sheila Smith & Jheri Walker

Foreword

The incarceration rate in our country has grown in alarming numbers. More and more people are finding themselves victim of this vicious cycle. Our youth comprises a large percent of America's confined. These youth are mostly uneducated and misdirected. However, if these same individuals were equipped with common sense and guidance most would have chosen an alternative path in life other than the path that has caused their present condition of misery and despair.

Experience can sometimes be our best teacher. With that in mind I wrote this book, a true account of my life experiences, not to glorify that lifestyle, but to expose some aspects of the challenges in life that youth of today are still confronted with. It is my hope that through this writing, some less fortunate youth who has made poor choices will become inspired to transform their thinking into a positive experience.

It is advantageous to adopt a mindset where hope exists for a brighter future in which you can rise above your present conditions rather than to become trapped in a negative cycle which will ultimately lead to imprisonment or some other sort of demise.

The prison system is filled with countless examples of both men and women who have made poor choices based on greed, ignorance or impatience. Don't become a victim of this cycle. Life is much too valuable.

Patience always edges out over difficult times. The only difference between one who is successful and one who fails, is not opportunity, but the burning desire to achieve at some point in life. Life is complex only if one perceives it. Failure occurs when you believe you have failed. Opportunity exists within your mind.

There are many lessons to be learned in life. Be wise, stay focused and learn from the mistakes of others. Now relax and take your mind on a journey with me.

Peace

Table of Contents

Chapter 1 One Winter Night...1

Chapter 2 City of Angels 9

Chapter 3 Orville Wright Jr. High..23

Chapter 4 Earning a Rep...33

Chapter 5 In Memory of Billy Dee 1977 47

Chapter 6 211 with a Vengeance..63

Chapter 7 Flashlight Therapy...77

Chapter 8 California State Prison..89

Chapter 9 San Quentin Prison 1980...101

Chapter 10 A Taste of Freedom 1985 113

Chapter 11 If These Walls Could Talk..119

Chapter 12 Leavenworth   Federal Prison 137

Chapter 13 USP Lewisburg 1988 155

Chapter 14 Aryan Brotherhood Reign of Terror..............................179

Chapter 15 Worst of the Worst- USP Marion 191

Chapter 16 Lompoc Revisited 205

Chapter 17 Club Fed 1993 215

Chapter 18 Looking Back June 1996 225

Chapter 19 El Monte Halfway House..243

Chapter 20 The Last Dance...257

Epilogue 269

About the Author..271

PROLOGUE

"Don't nobody move!" yelled the ski masked bandit as the other two bandits took their positions inside the bank.

Bandit number one hopped over the counter with bandit number two. Bandit number three stood watch in the lobby area.

"Who is the manager," barked bandit number one.

"I am!" replied the bank manager as if she had just gotten slapped.

"Get over there and get this vault open!" bandit number one commanded.

"I can't, it takes two keys to open it, the assistant manager has the other," the bank manager responded with pleading eyes.

"Stay down! Everyone stay down," bandit number three could be heard yelling in the lobby while nervously pacing back and forth.

"I'm telling you woman, get that vault open now!" bandit number one ordered as he displayed the semi-automatic handgun for assurance.

"I have the other key," the assistant manager stammered revealing his anonymity.

"You have ten seconds to open the vault, mister!" bandit number one said, sounding slightly desperate.

Both bandits entered the vault stuffing wrapped bundles of money into huge military style duffel bags.

"Thirty seconds!" bandit three yelled, indicating the time left to complete the mission. Generally, three minutes from the time a bank alarm is activated, the local police would respond to the call; unless other circumstances came into play.

"Five-0! Five-0! Hold 'em up," bandit three shouted to his confederates as he checked the activity of the police cruiser entering the parking area.

Unbeknownst to the bandits, every morning at the same time, a police cruiser made its rounds in the bank parking lot. Meticulous planning had been overlooked by the bandits.

An elderly woman waiting for her husband who had gone into the bank to withdraw funds, witnessed the ski masked bandits storm the bank. She ran towards the police cruiser frantically waving her hands.

"They're robbing the bank," the elderly woman screamed as she reached the police cruiser.

The police officer quickly radioed the dispatcher, "Robbery in progress, suspects wearing ski masks; send available units to Artesia and Hawthorne Boulevard."

The cruiser crawled toward the bank with caution.

"Let's go!"

"They're coming this way," the lookout said.

Inside the robbers realized their fate. The million dollar heist soured right before their eyes. Bandit number three, without much hesitation, darted out the North doors, never bothering to look back.

Bandit number one exchanged words with bandit number two, then bandit one also walked out the North doors, calmly removing his mask before he passed the exit. The bandit looked as inconspicuous as he possibly could.

Patrick Brown had been sitting at the intersection of Hawthorne and Artesia Boulevard. He was waiting for the stoplight to change. He noticed two men come out the bank, moments behind one another, both men wearing black, removing latex gloves. They seemed calm but cautious.

That's odd, he thought. He paid close attention.

Inside, bank teller Jones, watched the actions of bandit two frustratingly drag the second of two military duffel bags out of a side exit. Feeling safe enough, he took a closer look from the side exit glass. Bandit two loaded the duffel bags into the back of a Ford Bronco. The bandit who had now removed the mask gave Jones quite a surprise.

"That's no man," Jones noticed as bandit number two brushed the dark curls away from her eyes.

.

Chapter 1 One Winter Night

On a cold winter night, 18 January 1960, I was born at Memorial Hospital in Chicago, Illinois to the proud parents James and Elyse Lacy; I was the third child, the only boy, taking my name after my father.

We lived a typical family life on 79th and Union Streets, Chicago's Southside. A separation came early in my home, just before my fifth birthday. My mother and father who had not been getting along for reasons I did not understand parted ways.

My sisters and I moved in with our Gramps and Grandad during the divorce. We lived there in a red brick duplex home on 88th South Lowe Street. I attended Ryder Elementary School which sat cattycorner from where we lived. On our corner was a Mom & Pop store.

The African American family who owned the store resided on the upper floor of the market. Our family regularly shopped with them. The family who ran the store would extend credit to folks in the neighborhood based on their word to pay. A person's word was as good as gold in those days.

Our neighbors were the Williams' (Deborah, Calvin), Akins (Paul, Edward, Gregory, Darlene, Isaac), and Brumfield's (Lynette, Chubby, Brenda). We were a tight knit group of neighborhood kids.

It was not uncommon for us kids, eight and nine years old, to hang out on our front porch during a warm Chicago summer night until 11:00 or midnight where the heat was lingering inside homes making it impossible for restless kids to sleep.

We passed the night hours trying to count stars or playing silly porch games like; "Mother May I," "Simon Says" and occasionally someone would tell scary stories. During the day we played dodgeball, bottlecap, pitched pennies or Double Dutch jump rope with the girls.

We awkwardly turned over the jump rope after many clumsy attempts. I eventually got the hang of it, which gave me kudos with the girls, who ran in a very competitive pack.

There were block parties on Lowe Street during the summer. On holidays such as 4th of July, Memorial Day and Labor Day, bar-b-que grills lined the front yards of homes while adults grilled hamburgers, hot links and chicken.

Inside homes folks cooked baked beans, made potato salad, served chips, sodas and cold beer. Neighbors always had an open door policy on these festive holidays.

Music played over open amplifiers, playing what is considered today's golden oldies; artists such as the Spinners, Supremes, Temptations, Four Tops and Isley Brothers to name a few.

Near the hottest point of the day, adults would open the fire hydrant at the corner. The kids on the block, wearing swim wear or shorts, would stand under the gush of water, cooling down. They were memories never to be forgotten.

It was around the same time I nearly burned down our residence. Gramps was cooking breakfast for me one morning which consisted of cream of wheat, buttered toast and milk.

We had an oven that had a burner instead of flames. I was curious as to how the cream of wheat cooked without flames heating the pot.

Seeing that the burner on top the stove was red hot, steam coming out the pot was not enough to satisfy my curious mind. I took a piece of paper bag and held it on the burner.

Instantly a flame engulfed the piece of paper bag I was holding, causing me to drop it. I tried stomping out the paper but each time I stomped, the burning paper swooshed away from my feet.

The paper ended up in the pantry area on top of several grocery bags that were stored there. Panicking, I ran to the living room, dove on the couch, pretending to be asleep. A few minutes later someone smelled smoke. Family members alerted each other that there was a fire and we all scampered out of the house onto the front lawn.

Fire trucks raced to the scene as our kitchen went up in flames. Only the kitchen had been damaged. Thank God no one was hurt.

At this age living with Gramps and Grandad, I was in my most formative years. I learned from them values, compassion, and a sense of family, that I was too young to grasp in the hostile environment of my parents. It would not be revealed to me until I was an adult, by my mom, that Gramps was in fact my mother's oldest sister, Grandad her sister's husband. Gramps and Grandad were my grandparents, no one could tell me otherwise. We were family and that was all that mattered to me.

It was the only environment that I actually experienced guardians who were genuinely loving and supportive. Gramps and Grandad showered me and my sisters with much love and affection. We each had our own separate rooms. Every Christmas we were given an abundance of gifts. Ironically, one of my favorite gifts was a red fire truck that I could sit in to peddle. It had a large bell on top that rang loudly. I also sported a fireman's hat, roaring up and down the sidewalk I'd pretend there was some fire I was going to put out. Each year my world of fantasy play extended. I made sure Santa would get my requests.

"Gramps, do you think Santa would mind getting me a cowboy outfit?" I asked revealing young doe eyes.

"If you are good there is no telling what Santa may get you," Gramps responded.

"Well, could you ask him for me, please Gramps?" I asked in that familiar tone every child uses to charm unsuspecting grandparents.

Gramps was unaware that the Santa I was referring to was her. One snowy Christmas Eve I peered through a crack in the door with wide sparkly eyes as Gramps spread Christmas gifts around the evergreen Christmas tree. That Christmas I sported a cowboy suit with belt, boots, hat and two gun holsters.

"Bang! Bang! I got you, Grandad," I shouted in playful glee using the living room couch for cover, then running real fast almost slipping on the rug in the hallway, rolling into an adjacent room.

"The Indians are coming, stay down," I pretended letting off a barrage of make believe gunfire for the next half hour during the mock standoff.

While doing all the pretending and playing with neighborhood friends, I never really paid any attention to being away from my parents who were by now divorced.

"Get ready to take a bath and get dressed, your Dad is coming to get you," Gramps would tell me every so often.

"Aw, man," I whined aloud to no one in particular.

I consciously became sullen and withdrawn whenever my Dad came around. He would take me fishing, to the museum, or to buy school clothes. No matter what we did together I spoke very few words when around my Dad, so did he. I quietly feared the senior.

However, I did find a more loving bond with my Mom.

But, she had moved to California having remarried. She decided not to involve me and my sisters in the move because of our being enrolled in catholic school. Besides we were under good care with Gramps and Grandad.

I was aware that Mom was living in California where the Beverly Hillbillies lived. The fictional country family on television who had moved to Beverly Hills.

Whenever Mom phoned, I would swell with excitement.

"Hello, Momma."

"How you doing, son?"

"I'm doing fine Momma, I got an 'A' on my report card."

"That's good son, I'm really proud of you," she said approvingly.

"I drew some pictures for you too, Momma."

"You did?"

"Will you send them to Momma?"

"Yeah," I replied proudly.

It would not be until years later as I got older I started experiencing the effects of the absence of not being reared by my parents. I could sense there was some sort of family conflict.

"Gramps, when am I going to see Momma?" I began asking.

"Soon enough boy," Gramps answered.

"Okay," I said, never bringing it up again.

Some children who grow up without their biological parents tend to do poorly in school. I did. My father was informed of it. Instead of properly counseling me, he reacted by physically lashing out, punching me with his bare knuckled fist, as if I were a grown man and we were in a street brawl. I was nine years old.

Another time while playing with the Akins boys who lived next door, my father pulled up in the blue Pinto he drove, proceeded to beat me right there on the spot, in front of neighbors and all.

I frantically tried to elude my father's wrath running into the red brick home, while Dad pursued me, beating me with a belt. I failed to understand why so much anger had been directed towards me.

I felt that there were some underlying motive behind the beatings. The punches thrown too wildly, I wrote to my Mom in California in an attempt to seek refuge.

> Dear Momma,
>
> How are you doing? I'm fine. I was wondering if I could live with you in California? Please write me back soon and let me know.
>
> Check X on line. _Yes _No.
>
> P.S. I love you, Momma, xoxoxoxoxo.

Mom sent for me in a heartbeat. Maybe too soon for the man she had married, Leroy Adams. Catching the train alone to California I carried with me a neatly packed brown suitcase.

I was eager to reunite with my Mom. I was nine years old. Although not riding with an adult, the porters ensured that I had a safe trip, periodically checking on me at rest stops. The three day journey finally ended in the Amtrak station downtown Los Angeles.

My Mom, my sisters, and stepfather were there to pick me up in a brand new convertible Eldorado Cadillac.

"We got it made," I smiled inside.

Chapter 2 City of Angels

Our modest home sat in the View Park community also known as "The Hills" spacious homes built on or surrounded by hills. The neighborhood is situated between Baldwin Hills, Windsor Hills and Ladera Heights, all upscale affluent communities.

As the El Dorado Cadillac pulled onto 64th Street and Buckler, there were rows of manicured lawns. In front of the houses were clean sidewalks. Palm trees lined the blocks. A beautiful ivy garden led up the edge of our driveway ending near the porch. In our backyard were three fruit trees; lemon, orange and avocado. On the face it reminded me of a fantasy home. Yet, I was not aware of the hostilities that existed about me being an addition to the Adams household, nor was I aware that my alcoholic stepfather would become abusive.

Mom enrolled me in St. Bernadette's Catholic School in neighboring Baldwin Hills. I had the challenge of meeting a curriculum more advanced than previous schools I attended. My attention began to decline causing me to fall way behind the rest of the class. I eventually felt more comfortable getting into mischief.

Catholic schools are firm on discipline. My backside belonged to the class oak wood paddle for disobedient students. It had several air holes drilled into it for maximum effect.

It was a perverted sense of discipline developed long ago in someone's sadistic mind. The double pair of salt and pepper pants I wore to the ritual didn't suffice to ease the uncomfortable sting to my backside.

I didn't last a semester at St. Bernadette's. During a school carnival, two other kids and I who were set on mischief, knocked over carnival booths that were set up for games. My stepfather was called from work to pick me up due to me being immediately expelled for that incident. I waited in the Monsignor's office for my stepfather to pick me up. When he arrived, he proceeded to beat me with a belt inside the Monsignor's office out to his Eldorado Cadillac. I was grounded for thirty days to room restriction, no television, and no outdoors. It felt like I was banished to some remote island or jail.

During prison stints, while in isolation for extended periods, I often reflected on those periods of me being grounded as a child. Doing so may have equipped me mentally to endure the pressures of long term isolation.

My behavior at school was attributed to the abuse I felt at home. I strongly believed that because I was not Leroy Adam's biological son, was the reason that I was the recipient of that abuse in the Adam's household.

There was also physical abuse towards my mother which I felt hopeless to intervene. The drunken arguments were loud and mentally annoying, keeping me up most of the night, frightened.

On more than one occasion my stepfather pulled a gun on my Mom, threatening to kill her as I looked on stunned. Living at the Adam's residence was dismal at best. At a young age I spiraled downward in regards to building social skills.

After getting expelled from St. Bernadette School, my mother enrolled me in 54th Street School. I was within walking distance from the public school which sat on 54th and Rimpau Boulevard. 54th Street School started at grades four through six. The student's recreation period consisted of kick ball, dodgeball, caram boards and tether ball. Kickball is a ghetto version of softball. A pitcher on a mound rolls a brown soccer type ball to the kicker upon request of how he or she wanted it rolled.

"Give me bouncies," one would say, indicating they wanted the ball to be rolled in small or big bounces. "Roll it hard and fast" another kicker might request.

Sam Williams reigned as the school's kickball champion. Standing over 6 ft in the sixth grade, Sam would kick the ball over the fence in the huge playground virtually every time he stepped to the plate. Years later, Sam Williams, became a professional basketball player with the NBA, playing center for the Golden State Warriors and other teams.

At the time, grade schools experienced very little gang activity. However, it was a year after Raymond Lee Washington founded the Crips Street Gang.

The Crips eventually became one of the biggest street gangs in Los

Angeles. Prior to the influx of gangs on school yards, there was what was called "King of the school." The king of a particular school was in comparison to a reigning boxing champion. Young men with quick hands or power punches ruled the school yard until another challenger felt he could take that title. A duel would be set.

At 54th Street School, Carlos Powers, a light skinned, wiry framed sixth grader, who sported a huge silky afro, held this title undisputedly until he was challenged. Phillip Ricks, a short and stocky, dark skinned youth fought a grueling battle with Carlos in the gulley, a secluded area a mile from the school. To the students of 54th Street School, the fight was comparable to an Ali/Frazier fight. The next day Carlos sported a shiner to school, evidence that Phillip was the new "King of school". It was news at the grade school for many years. Until some other gossip was worthy of reporting.

Although I was not there to witness the fight at the gulley, there was one other I did see, the one which I was one of the main participants. One sunny afternoon during lunch period, I was hanging around the fence area waiting for the bell to ring signaling the end of lunch. A cute, dark skinned girl approached me casually with small talk.

"Hi! What's your name?" she said.

"Are you new to this school?" she smiled flirtatiously.

Being naturally shy, I stumbled on my words, "Yeah, um, I'm sort of new I guess. My name is James," I managed to say with a dry throat.

"Well, nice meeting you," she said hurrying off, responding to the bell that just rung for class.

"Oh, I'm Tammy," she chimed before disappearing.

I headed back to class spellbound, thinking about the mysterious girl I just met. I was abruptly confronted by a curly head sixth grader named Stuff.

"I saw you talking to my girlfriend, we gotta fight. Meet me after school," he said without leaving me any recourse.

The dreamy spell I was in turned nightmarish. I tried to discern how I suddenly ended up in a duel over a girl I just met seconds ago. By last period I watched the clock on the wall vigilantly. For some odd reason time seemed to fly.

My classmates began to taunt me, "What you gonna do?" they asked.

"Don't worry about what I'm gonna do," I lashed out. Wishing I could just disappear.

Funny things happen to us on school grounds growing up as kids. It is some of those experiences that form a mindset of how we will react in similar situations as we mature into adults.

The school bell rang ending the day. It was the time of day when children's energy level rose, joyous that another school day was over. To my ears, the sound of the bell was the beginning of a boxing mismatch, one I wanted no part of. Maybe I could leave from the other side of the school I reasoned.

As the students filed out of their classes, I could hear several of them talking among each other.

"There's gonna be a fight," one said.

"Where, when?" students with inquiring minds wanted to know.

I lingered around the classroom fiddling with my books, trying to be the last one out. I started small talk with why homeroom teacher.

"Ms. Keifer, what was that homework assignment again?" stalling as long as I could.

After she explained the homework, I walked out of class, sure that all the kids were well on their way home. Seeing the hallway empty, I started my journey home feeling relieved.

As I walked down the block I could see a huge crowd of kids at the corner, milling around. I knew they were waiting for me because I was the last student out of the building.

As I neared the crowd, my palms started to sweat, my throat also became dry. I was unsure how the fight might turn out. I thought of a million and one ways to get out of it.

Stuff was in the center of the group and kids were shifting around him restlessly. I attempted to walk pass the crowd as if I didn't know what was going on. I was stopped dead in my tracks.

"Let's get 'em up; we gotta fight," Stuff said.

"I don't want to fight you man," I responded having rehearsed it a zillion times in my head as if it were the magic words that would set me free from the swarm of blood thirsty youth.

Stuff and I went through the antics of knock this stick off my shoulder, cross this line, and so on, to which I proved to be an unwilling participant. Finally and without warning, Stuff threw a punch that caught me square on my nose. I had been still holding onto my school books. They scattered everywhere as I fell to the pavement. Stuff got on top me, pummeling with a flurry of blows.

A woman driving by who noticed the fight stopped her car and began yelling,

"You kids break it up, go home; stop all of this nonsense."

It was all she needed to say for the crowd of hyper kids to disperse. The woman then helped me up. "Hold your head up, it will stop the bleeding," she said.

My nose that had been busted was running like a faucet. I took my half torn shirt, held it to my nose, and walked home. Declining the ride that the woman had offered. It would be the last time I would let someone sucker punch me.

The situation at home with my stepfather grew worse. There was an arrangement made for me to move to San Antonio, Texas to live with my father's mother, Grandmother Thorton, Uncle Michael and Aunt Bonnie. A year later I moved back to Chicago where I lived with my mother's best friend Lydia Mitchum and her sons; Tommy, Andy, Raphael and Cameron. The residence was at 80th Street and Woodlawn Avenue. I attended St. Felicitas Catholic School. After graduating from the eighth grade I returned back to Los Angeles, California where all was well. So I thought.

◆ ◆ ◆

It was June 1973. School was out. I was at my so called home on 64th and Buckler in Los Angeles, California. It was during that summer I started making small change cutting lawns in the neighborhood. Using my stepfather's lawn mower and edger, my neighbor, Alvin and I, would go up to houses revealing poster boy smiles asking if we could cut their lawn for five dollars.

We earned up to fifteen dollars a weekend, then splurged on pizza, movies, ice cream and spent several hours at the pinball arcade. After a day of arcade fun, we'd hang out at the McLendon's, who also lived on our block.

Dean and Michelle were like extended family members to me. I'd spend hours at their home listening to records and watching television. Other friends on our block included; Chuckie, Tory, Celeste, Phyllis and Freddie.

We were generally an average group of kids in search of good fun. None of us drank nor smoked marijuana. Every now and then someone older would light up a Kool cigarette. I made several attempts at smoking but always ended up coughing my head off. I always had to be in the house before the street lights came on. If I missed by one minute Mom would be on the front porch yelling for me. James! James! No matter how far down the block I went, I always instinctively heard her call.

In between hanging out at the McLendons, I would spend time around the corner with Brian and Keith Spencer. Both were four years my senior. I would help them deliver newspapers and they would tell me war stories about the Crips. The Crips were wreaking havoc across Crenshaw Boulevard.

Others who hung out at Spencer's were; Skull, White Mouse, Michael Hamilton, Gary Patton, Willis Vaughn, Curtis Hood, Carla, and Motor Mouse. We were a laid back crew who represented "Crip." I was the youngest. Willis Vaughn, an elder, coined the term — "Hills Crips." We set a standard for the next generation which now refers to that area as "The Overhill," a faction of Neighborhood Rolling Sixties.

As a teenager I heard a lot of legendary stories about Raymond Washington and Big Tookie, Crip leaders, who would go into enemy territory beating down their rivals.

Another legendary story takes place at the Los Angeles Palladium where concerts are held. As the story goes, some Crip members approached a group of teens depriving them of their leather coats. At the time, leather jackets were popular among teens symbolizing a fashion statement of the era. One of the young men, Robert Ballou, defiantly refused to give his jacket to the Crips. In an unfortunate set of circumstances, the gang beat the young man down, stomping him to death while they whistled like birds, Crip whistling.

The incident caused a media frenzy within the city of Los Angeles about the notorious group of teens calling themselves Crips. Their gang attire was tan or grey khaki suits and Stacy Adams Bisquits. They also sported an earring in their left ear.

Crips also wore starched Levi jeans, Chuck Taylor All Stars and Pendleton shirts. The gang traveled in packs like predatory wolves, vamping on rival gang members.

The legendary Crip originals, Barefoot Pookie, Big Bamm, Buddah, Tookie and others set into motion a span of disorganized violence that dominates Los Angeles' gang turf 'til this day. Their motto; *"Crips don't die, we multiply."*

Crippin in the early years wasn't all gangsterism and violence. There was also a sense of unity and family. Chilling at Sportsman Park, St. Andrew's Park, Will Rogers Park and Centinela Park where all Crip factions gathered to smoke weed, drink wine, and listen to the sounds of the Isley Brothers, Ohio Players, Earth, Wind & Fire and the Parliment Funkadelic.

By 1976 most of the Crip originals were falling back, letting the younger Crips grab the infamy, which eventually took gangbanging to another level.

When young black males come from broken homes where there is no male figure in that home to learn from, those young males become prone to emulating their peers who have a stronger influence over them than their families.

They see the gang as family, one of cohesiveness and strength; elements that are lacking in their homes. The young black male will gravitate towards this structure even though it consists of negative behavior.

The African American family over time has deteriorated, evidence that this breakdown has attributed to the influences of gang and criminal lifestyles among our youth.

Brian, Keith and I would eventually venture out to Keniston Avenue, about seven blocks from the hills, where we hung out over the Smith's. At the Smith's, Big Helen, Billy, Sheila and Tracy lived in a single parent home.

Their mother worked two jobs. The residence turned into Satan's den when Ms. Smith was away. Loud music, drinking, reefer smoking, sex and sometimes fights were the norm. It was night and day in comparison to hanging out at the McLendon's.

There was never a boring moment at the Smith's. The most positive thing about the Smith's home was that it was a retreat from the streets. Although it was an all day affair, there were some house rules. Big Helen, the oldest, laid down the law. Big Helen weighed every bit of three hundred pounds. It's only fair to say it seemed as if she did.

Big Helen kept things from getting too out of control. She held the position as guardian of the coup. Helen carried her own despite the ruthlessness of some of the neighborhood Crips who frequented regularly. Stacy Bullock, Stagolee, TQ, Dennis Pinkey, Jheri Walker, Milky and many more were regulars.

I befriended Helen's brother, Billy, who was a year older than me, but a lot wilder. We were both getting more and more out of control each day, we were a match made in heaven. Billy's sister, Sheila, who was one year younger than me, was my first love. A mutual attraction developed at first sight.

Sheila and I were attracted to each other like minks, our hormones taking full control of our bodies. I was barely fourteen years old. Sheila and I spent nights together in the back house, a room adjacent to the house. We'd spend hours of blissful lovemaking, cuddling into the wee hours of the night.

Afterwards, I'd hurry home through the darkness of the L.A. streets, creeping back through my bedroom window, falling fast asleep. Sheila was my tender experience, soft and supple. Our lovemaking was on the horizon. As our teenage lust grew, we became inseparable.

The bond between me and my homie grew even stronger. Billy was a young thief and ladies man. Together we would prowl the neighborhood stealing cars then joyriding in them listening to 1580 K-day doing donuts, screeching tires and making clouds of thick smoke in the air.

We drove around in stolen cars that we kept for weeks, as if we actually owned them, picking up females and sexing them in the back seat. Of course, they would have no idea the car was stolen. That was our idea of fun under the California sun.

On more than one occasion, I would get caught riding in one of the g-rides. I would have to spend months in Los Padrinos or Central Juvenile Hall until the case was adjudicated. I was usually placed in a Boy's home. Kicking it over the Smith's, introduced me to the hard knocks of street life.

James Lacy

Chapter 3 Orville Wright Jr. High

September school session arrived; I had spent the entire summer on Keniston Avenue in an attempt to escape the boredom of the middle class area at the Adams residence.

My mother enrolled me in the ninth grade at Orville Wright Jr. High, where I would experience racism firsthand. Wright Jr. High was located in the all white community of Westchester, four miles from Playa del Rey beach.

African Americans were bussed there from urban areas. African Americans were a very small percent of the student body, but we were rapidly growing. There had been occasional racial incidents on and off campus due to blacks integrating into the school.

After enrolling in Orville Wright, I noticed I was far more advanced street wise than most students, having spent the summer under Billy's tutelage. Set out on rebellion, I vented anger that would set a pattern of delinquency at the Jr. High.

I met another Crip at the school who went by the name, Kojack. Kojack was fourteen years old and a stocky two hundred pounds. He sported a clean shaven bald head, years before it became popular among black youth. We met under circumstances that developed a friendship between us on and off campus.

I came strolling through class one morning pulling up on a student who was sitting down minding his own business.

"Give me your wallet," I say to him.

"No, I'm not giving you anything," he answers defiantly.

I grab him by the collar, this dude gets up and he's like 6'2", 220 pounds towering over me. I'm thinking, oh shit! I punch him anyway, he lunges at me, I duck. From out of nowhere, Kojack, who I never met up until this point is on the guy's back punishing him. I counter with punches from the front. The big guy is swinging like a trapped bear.

I snatch his back pocket, ripping it from his pants; his wallet falls to the floor. By this time the teacher intervenes ordering me and Kojack from the class. Kojack introduces himself to me claiming to be from Five-Six Syndicate Crip.

Kojack was a serious and loyal Crip. However, he was not a validated Five-Six Crip. Some Five-Six Syndicate Crips caught Kojack strolling through Ladera Park on Halloween night, asking him what set he was from, "Five-Six Syndicate," he responded. He immediately received a thorough beat down that put him in the hospital. Kojack fell back from Crippin a couple of years, but ended up starting his own faction -- Tenth Avenue Crips.

On another occasion, I took a wannabe's bomber jacket. Bomber jackets were worn by pilots during wartime. Puffy jackets with synthetic fur around the collar. The jacket became a symbol among Crip members. If wearing one, others automatically assumed you were Crip.

The teen who was wearing the jacket was Brian Sprinkles, a Crip wannabe. He was not a Crip, but wanting to be one. Creating a situation to punk Brian and expose his hand, I approached him during lunch period.

"Say cuzz. What size jacket is that you're wearing?"

"I dunno," he answered meekly.

"Can I try it on?" I asked, hiding the deception in my voice.

"Yeah, sure," he complied, then taking the jacket off handing it to me.

"Thanks cuzz, it fits just fine," I said, changing the expression on my face to a scary mask as I walked away sporting the new jacket.

I learned these strong arm tactics while living with my gramps in Chicago. I'd attempt to go into the corner store which was also a hangout for the Black Stone Rangers. Weasel, an old head, would stop me and say, "Give me a quarter little man."

"I don't have one," I'd say.

"Well, what's this in your pocket?" Weasel asked shaking me down.

"I'm going to the store for my gramps."

"I don't care. Give me that change," Weasel insisted.

After the first couple times, I got wise hiding the money in my tennis shoes. Weasel stopped me for a shakedown finding no money. I walked past him wearing a shit-eating grin.

Behind the coat incident at Wright Jr. High, Steve Welch, an up and coming hoodster who was good with his fists, approached me during recess and confronted me about the jacket I took from Brian.

"Hey man, you got my friend's jacket?" Steve asked.

"Yeah, I got it," I said, my fist balled up eyes squinting for a rumble."

"Well, he wants it back," Steve said, feeling for a hint of fear in my reaction.

"Since you are in the business of delivering messages, tell your friend it's mine now and if he wants it to come and get it himself," I shot back looking directly into Steve's eyes, not flinching.

"Yeah, whatever man," Steve responded.

I respected Steve for approaching me man to man in an attempt to get his friend's jacket back despite me having a reputation for being affiliated with the Crips, who would make appearances after school intimidating kids with their stares and hitting on cuties. Had it not been for that, Steve Welch would have probably given me a squabble more than I could bargain for.

Yet, in those times, one did not take back something he did or said. It showed cowardice. Not returning the jacket showed there was not a scared bone in my body. Steve also acknowledged the cool defiance I displayed in his attempt to pull my card. Out of that situation grew a bond of camaraderie that would last for many years. Steve became my Crip comrade and best friend.

It seems that when you are on top of your game everything else falls in place, especially with a little bit of manipulation.

Rinnnng....Rinnnnng...Rin

"Hello!"

"Hello, may I speak with James Lacy, please?" the sweet voice asked.

"Speaking."

"Hi James, this is Kim."

"Kim? You mean as in Kimberly, Kim-ber-ly Reeves? Fine ass!"

"Boy, please! Yeah, Kim," she answered in a *my shit don't stink* attitude.

"How did you get my number and what brings you to call, *Ms. Hard to Get?*"

"Well, you took my friend's jacket, that's messed up," Kim stated,

27

sounding as if she had some personal interest.

"Why is that?" I asked, irritated to the bone over people asking me about the damn jacket.

"That jacket is Crip attire, Brian ain't no Crip," I said trying not to reveal the jealousy in my voice.

"Besides, if he really wanted it, he would not have let me take it from him. But look here Kim, I ain't trying to spend time on the phone talking about another dude. My mom has to use the phone, so, can you call back some other time?"

I knew in my heart that it wasn't all about the jacket, but all the notoriety and the ruckus I had stirred up as a new student on the small junior high school campus.

I was of interest to the sheltered, spoiled girl from the affluent Windsor Hills community. She was attracted to my mischievous attitude wanting to get to know me personally.

We started phoning each other regularly. Throughout my frequent stays in juvenile hall, Kim would write me. She was the only female I'd ever been intimidated by, due to her family's wealth, her infallible beauty, and model looks.

However, at the time, Crippin was more of an interest to me than becoming involved in a complex teenage relationship, as Kim was intent on making it. Kim, stood her ground for me to make a choice between the lifestyle I was living or everything I wanted in her. Well, more often than not, when you are young, you are foolish. I wasn't giving up Crippin for anything.

Sometime later during the school year at Orville Wright, a large group of black students, myself included, were returning from lunch off campus. We were confronted by a group of white students and residents of the Westchester community.

We always traveled in groups to and from lunch because of past racial agitation and skirmishes. This particular afternoon, the whites taunted us with racial slurs.

"Get out of here niggers, stay in your own neighborhoods," the angry whites yelled without any justification other than hate.

"Fuck you, honkie!" some scared individual in our group yelled back without stepping up.

Before we had time to react, a former Orville Wright student known for his racial hatred, walked up on the four of us with the mob behind him.

"That's Jeff Webster!" Darryl Jones said, sounding like a teenage girl as we faced them.

Jeff Webster spoke first looking me directly in my eyes. "What was that you niggers were saying?" he said, his face contorting with hate.

The blacks on the opposite side of the fence gawked. Their faces revealing fear of the old slave. I caught glimpses out of the corner of my eye of whites who were hyped up for action, as if us black students were from another planet.

Clearly, they were following Jeff Webster's lead, ready to unleash at his call. I stood my ground though.

"It wasn't any of us here who said anything. If it was me, I would not hesitate to repeat it."

For reasons unknown, Jeff stood down.

"The next time you niggers come through here mouthing off, you won't get far."

We stood silent, but defiantly. Prideful that we did not run like the other cowards.

As we returned to school, Steve turned asking me, "How come you didn't run like the rest of them?"

"Come to my locker, I'll show you."

Looking both ways first, I pulled out a snub nose .38 revolver from my waistband, then put it in my locker. Steve let out a low whistle.

"Maan! Where did you get that?" he asked excitedly.

"It's my step father's. He keeps it under his mattress. I saw him hide it there. When he goes to work I pack it," I said proudly.

I will admit, carrying the weapon when the angry white mob confronted us, gave me a sense of security. Although I never anticipated using it, knowing I had it gave me the courage I needed.

Later in the week, I was summoned to the principal's office. Word had gotten around that I was packing a gun to school. Mainly because I kept showing it off. As the principal interrogated me in his office about the gun, school security searched my locker, but failed to produce a weapon. In an unprecedented act they expelled me from school anyway.

By the time I had made it home that afternoon, my mother had already been informed of the incident. She went on an angry tirade.

"Boy, I do everything I can to see that you do the right thing, and you always seem to do the wrong things."

"I ain't done nothin, Momma," I whined.

"That's your problem boy, you never do anything wrong," she lectured as I had already tuned her out.

During the time I had been expelled, emotions ran high at home. My mother and I separated from the Adams residence again. Mom rented a two bedroom apartment on 104th and Woodworth Avenue in Inglewood. While we were moving into the apartment, the only thing I was thinking was that we were moving into a Bloods' neighborhood. Just my luck, I thought.

Chapter 4 Earning a Rep

Morningside High School sat on 104th Street and Yukon Avenue, directly across the street from our small apartment. Morningside campus started at grade nine through twelve. I was new to the campus, which handicapped me from the celebrity like status I enjoyed at Orville Wright Junior High.

At Morningside High, I was up against hardcore gang members of The Undertaker Family headed by Johnny Sutton. They were a spinoff of The Inglewood Family gang of Inglewood, California.

Although young and outnumbered by the older Bloods, I still harbored an open disregard for their existence. I was not supposed to like them. They were my rivals. Yet, I had never been faced with any of them until now.

The stories were passed down through generations, Bloods are our enemies. If you get caught slipping in their hoods, you'd get beat down or even killed. The Bloods hear the same stories about Crips, which makes the possibility of a truce bleak.

On the very first day of school, I sported Crip attire; Stacy Adams bisquits, starched Levi jeans with one inch cuffs, Charlie Brown shirt, blue bomber jacket and a cross earring hanging from a two inch chain in my left ear. I represented to the fullest.

During the lunch period as students gathered in the quad area, I decided to make my appearance. I had learned from the originals that Crips don't downplay their existence. You don't hide from the enemy. Show, no fear.

Not knowing one single person at the school, I reached down in my heart and strolled through the quad area, where the Bloods hung out during lunch. I felt like a peacock showing off his colors. It was a bold affront to the Bloods, blatant disrespect.

Although there were no direct challenges from the males, it was actually some of the young women who seemed infuriated by my boldness.

"We don't allow Crips at this school," an anonymous female shouted.

"Blood here," another female said.

No one actually confronted me as I strolled through the quad defiantly, not intimidated the least. But of course I was strapped that day.

During the following week, I got comfortable, resorting to strong arming again. Seeing two marks, I stopped them.

"Come here you two. Show me the insides of your pockets," I said, revealing a face I wore to intimidate.

The pair's compliance reassured me that, although in a tougher environment, I could still prevail on some level. That Friday afternoon at the football team's school pep rally in the gymnasium, while the soulful tune of the Average White Band, *"Only a School Boy Crush"* played, I started flashing gang signs, throwing up the "C" while Coco was Crip walking.

There were a handful of Crips at the school besides Coco. Money Mike, from Imperial Village Crip and who eventually became a Neighborhood Sixties, Big CW (aka Charles Williams) also from the Neighborhood Sixties, Tank, Woobie, Monty from 108th Street Crips, and a few others.

The Bloods, who were sitting in the opposite bleachers, felt they had seen enough of me dissing them.

"Let's pull this dude up after the rally," Larry Sutton, younger brother of the leader of the UT Family said.

Unbeknownst to the plot building against me, I continued throwing up the set, called representing. Some of the students sitting next to me concerned about my actions cautioned me, "Say man, you can't be doing that here, the Bloods will smash you."

"So what," I responded back.

"It's Crippin on mines."

The rally ended and the students filed out the gym. As I walked out, I was immediately confronted by Larry Sutton, and seven angry Bloods. As they surrounded me, Larry started removing his jacket.

"You disrespecting us Bloods, me and you going head up," he said.

I doubted the fight would go heads up. There are no codes in gang warfare. Everything is fair when you are trying to win. Although I did find the challenge threatening, I would just take my beating.

It's part of the game. They catch you out of pocket; you catch them out of pocket. What comes around goes around. You don't eat cheese.

At about the same time I had mentally prepared myself for a beat down, two elder Crips who had watched the whole scenario from afar approached the scene.

"What's up cuzz, you aight?" one of the Crips said, saving me from a beat down.

"These fools are trippin, cuz. I don't know what's up," I said.

"It ain't gonna be no tripping, I just want to go head up," Larry interjected; knowing once the rumble started it wasn't going down like that.

A crowd started to form and it was only that the two Crips were respected that the situation did not turn into a mob scene. A security guard who noticed the gathering of the group of students and sensing trouble, walked over.

"Break it up, move along, go home," he said.

The crowd broke off. The two elder Crips and I walked towards the back gate. The Bloods followed closely like hyena predators waiting for a sign of weakness. In this instance for the elders to part.

"You got a lot of heart youngster," one of the Crips said who hadn't even introduced themselves.

"There are more Crips in this school than you think, but they stay in their place."

"Righteous on that, good looking," I said.

You'd think it would have been some sort of omen. Not hardly. I was surely trying to earn a rep at all costs. It signified who you were. Without one, you were just another Joe.

Later that night, I caught the bus back into the hood on Keniston Avenue. I kept close ties with the homies no matter where we moved. Keniston was my home away from home. I related the incident between me and the Bloods to Billy, Stacy and Jheri. They wanted to retaliate. We combed the Morningside area in a g-ride, strapped, but without a clue as to where Sutton and his boys lived. We retreated back to Keniston Avenue and drank crazy 8 (Old English 800) beer, all night.

The next day was quiet. No sighting of Sutton and his boys. The homies left me with a .22 caliber long nose pistol that would ensure that all went well. The next day as school was letting out, a friend and I attempted a short cut across the football field, where the Morningside

Monarchs were scrimmaging. The Monarchs, the official name for the athletic squads, consisted mainly of Bloods members. Some were the same that had confronted me at the rally. Probably thinking there goes that Crip again. Someone shouted, "Hey you! Get the fuck off our field."

"Fuck you fool, this is Crip," I responded.

A few of the Bloods started running towards us. I reached for the pistol that was in my waistband. Raising it in the air, I pulled the trigger.

"Pop, pop, pop, pop, pop," the gun screamed.

"Ca--Ca--Carip," I shouted as I saw the Bloods' faces eat dirt.

I handed the gun to my friend as we walked through the gate, me first. No sooner than I walked through, Inglewood Police driving an unmarked vehicle quickly apprehended me.

"You hold it right there."

The detective stopped me because I was first out the gate. My friend was walking a little distance behind me as if we were not together.

"Put your hands on the hood of the car," the cop ordered.

After a pat down search the detective ordered me to empty my pockets and put the contents on the hood of the police vehicle. Four .22 caliber shells rolled around on the hood.

"What did you do with the gun?" he asked.

"What gun?" I answered.

"Maybe you will figure it out after a few days in juvenile hall," the detective said manhandling me while he put me in the back seat of the unmarked police car.

Not hardly, I thought. I knew it was ludicrous to tell on one self as well as socially unacceptable to tell on your friend. Going to juvenile hall was not as bad as it seemed. There were other youth there from all over the County of Los Angeles who rebelled in the community, home, or school. I worried little when I spent months at Los Padrinos, Wayside or Central Juvenile Hall.

"I see you have been to your home away from home again," Sheila would tease whenever I would get out.

Between turning corners with Billy, and going to the halls, Sheila and I found time to engage in steamy sex. Making love to soulful tunes like Smokey Robinson's *"Agony and Ecstasy"* or the Moments *"Come on Sexy Momma."*

Back on the street again, after a couple months in juvey, due to lack of evidence, I went back to Morningside High School. No more problems with the Bloods. Although I don't remember doing homework, I was passed to the tenth grade.

The greatest educational setback there has ever been in our society is African American youth being passed through elementary, middle and high schools of America, failing to get a formal education. As a whole, this leads to an imbalance in our society and also within the African American family structure.

During their rocky road marriage, my mother reconciled with Mr. Adams, and we were off again, back to the Overhill residence, where it would be another tumultuous year.

I had to transfer over to Westchester High School, a school comprised of mostly Orville Wright Jr. High graduates—spoiled kids who drove to school in Mercedes Benzes, Audi's, Volvo's and other luxury cars, flaunting their wealth. There were several teen actors who attended Westchester High. In middle and high schools in America, some kids go to the extreme trying to impress their peers or be like them.

I toned it down a little while attending Westchester, keeping my out of control behavior limited to after school hours. I befriended a young woman named Krystle; we shared a seat on the bus together during the ride to and from school.

Krystle was cute, bronze complexioned, with smooth skin and a million dollar smile. It did not take long for us to bond with one another. We exchanged numbers and talked on the phone every night. We seemed to have a lot in common. We found solace in our friendship. Krystle and I were not romantically involved. We just grew as friends. Although Sheila was my first love, Krystle was my first female friend, someone with whom I could be me. We would openly confide in one another. But in my neighborhood I was becoming a different person.

Billy, Stacy, Jheri and I were getting quite a reputation in and around our neighborhood. We were always trying to outdo each other to see who could be the craziest.

I earned the nickname Crazy Warlock by now and a reputation that went with it. I even fooled myself into believing that I was really crazy. Due to all the notoriety we were getting, the Neighborhood Crips across Crenshaw Boulevard were taking notice. Since our turfs neighbored, they wanted the handful of us Crips to merge with them.

A meeting was called by Baby Face; an articulate, charismatic gang leader repping for the Neighborhood Sixties Crips. The meeting was held at Ladera Community Park in our neighborhood "The Hills".

Other Neighborhood Crips were there: Baby Huey, Big Rick, Herman Moncrief, Fred (Snoop Dog) Hill and Slu. Representing our hood was: Kevin (Big Cat) Ducette, Stacy Bullock, Billy Smith, Floyd (Motor Mouse) Nelson, Crazy Kat, Jheri Walker and me. The joining of our turfs in 1975 created one of the largest uninterrupted gang turfs in the city of Los Angeles. We were the Rolling Sixties Neighborhood Crips.

Billy, Stacy, Jheri and I stepped up our antics, riding through rival neighborhoods that bordered us we'd confront enemies.

"Hey homies, what set ya'll from?"

"Inglewood Family, here!" they would reply.

"Crip, here!" we'd say jumping out the g-ride and commence to beating them down.

One night while jamming at a house party near Baldwin Hills, Billy, Jheri and I were chillin' to the hippest tunes when we were interrupted by Stacy. Stacy had an altercation with a member of the Black Stones.

"Get ready to leave homies. I got into it with one of the Black Stones. I'm turning this party out."

Stacy had just ruined my evening with the brown skinned cutie I had just met at the party. I was in the process of finessing her into the back seat of our g-ride for a moment of passion.

"I gotta take care of something, girl; let me get back with you," I said, not even having time to get her digits.

We all met at the six-five Chevy and Stacy pulled out a sawed off .22 rifle from under the seat.

The girl who hosted the party had been looking out the window finding it odd that we left so soon. As she did, shots rang out in succession.

Rat, a tat, tat, tat, tat, tat, tat, echoed through the still night air. The slamming of doors and screeching tires indicating we had fled. Driving through the city streets, we retreated back to Keniston Avenue where we spent the remainder of the night drinking wine and smoking reefer.

"Pass me that bottle, cuzzin," Jheri said, as we drank Mad Dog 20/20 wine.

The following Monday detectives drove to Westchester High School with a warrant for me. I was taken away in handcuffs. The detectives wanted to question me about the shooting. The girl who gave the party knew me from school. She saw me standing under the street light with the others as shots rang out. Aside from that incident, a criminal complaint had been filed against me by a student claiming that I had strong armed him at school.

I was taken to Los Padrinos Juvenile Hall where some months later I was deemed a menace to society due to having racked up several criminal offenses within a short period of time. A juvenile court judge sentenced me to Camp Community Placement as an incorrigible youth.

The juvenile justice system intends on rehabilitating youth before they embark upon a career of crime. However, at that time, among Los Angeles' gang subculture doing time was considered a badge of honor.

I was sent to Camp Karl Holton in San Fernando Valley, situated about sixty miles outside of Los Angeles. Camp Holton, one of several youth facilities in Southern California, was the only co-ed youth camp in Los Angeles County. It served as an educational and rehabilitation center. The facility was surrounded by a 12ft. high brick wall.

At Camp Karl Holton, teenagers did most everything with the females. We ate in the dining room side by side, walked the yard together, attended the same classes at school and there were even dances held once a month in one of the dorm units. When a slow jam played, we were allowed to slow dance, but a distance between gyrating hips was enforced. The counselors were like referees with hawk eyes monitoring the sexual youthful energy in the confines of the dimly lit gymnasium.

"You're getting too close," the counselors would say.

I met a girl there named Susan. We called her Susie Q. She was beautiful, honey complexioned, with green eyes, and sandy brown hair down to her ass. She was considered my girlfriend; although it was more of a platonic relationship.

Some of the other youth I bonded with at Camp Holton were; Roberta from Hoover, Stix, Gata from Barrio Grape Street Watts, Lisa (Payasa), from Eighteenth Street and Joe Rob from Athens Park Boys.

The daily schedule at Camp Karl Holton consisted of group counseling sessions in the evenings and educational programming during the day. To graduate from Camp Karl Holton it was mandatory to participate in these programs.

A point system was implemented to ensure the youth at the camp maintained their best behavior. These points reflected everything from attitude, the making of your bed, and program participation. So many points were even required to go to the commissary to be able to purchase chips, sodas or cookies.

You lived by the points, died by the points. The usual period of confinement in juvenile camp was normally six months maximum. Those who did not conform to the rules maxed out at up to twelve months.

Pumping weights, playing basketball, softball and letter writing were some of the leisure activities youth did while awaiting our return to society. Unable to graduate after six months, because of unruly behavior I decided finally to conform to camp rules. It was not until nine months after I had been committed to Camp Karl Holton that I was released.

It was the summer of 1977 when Mom picked me up from Camp Holton to bring me home. I was seventeen years old, pumped up from weight lifting and darker from the scorching San Fernando Valley sun. It was the year *"Wishing on a Star"* by Rolls Royce, *"Brick House"* by the Commodores, *"Flashlight"* by Parliment Funkadelics, were all at the top of R&B charts.

During the ride home I thought about seeing my girlfriend Sheila. I could not wait to see her. Gotta find a way to get Moms car, I contemplated.

I had seen my last days at the Overhill residence. Mom pulled up to a location unfamiliar to me. While I was away at Camp Holton, Mom moved into a modest home on 70th Street and Halldale Avenue. It was the neighborhood of the Eight Trey Gangster Crips.

Chapter 5 In Memory of Billy Dee 1977

Back in the day all Crip factions were allies. The Eight Trey Gangsters were not yet a rival faction. In fact, Rolling Sixties and Eight Trey went on missions together against enemy Bloods, the Vaness Gangsters and Inglewood Family Gang. The new generation of Crips has drawn lines all over South Central Los Angeles into war zones, where every set has an enemy lurking. Crip sets against each other, against Blood sets, too. Drive by shootings occur on a regular basis.

The first person I met after settling into my new residence was Gangster Brown, an Eight Trey Gangster Crip. I still had my camp clothes on: blue denim jeans, blue denim shirt with Camp Holton stenciled in large black letters on the back, brown brogan boots and my hair picked out into a huge afro. I was sporting seventeen inch arms.

"Hey cuzz, where you from?" Gangster Brown asked.

"I'm from Rolling Sixties, cuzz," I responded eyeing him closely not sure what to expect next.

"I'm from Eight Trey Gangster, they call me Gangster Brown," he said smiling.

"You stay here, cuzz?" he asked, indicating the house we were standing in front of.

"Yeah," I answered, "My Mom moved here while I was in camp. I just came home today."

"Is that right, cuzz?" Brown remarked as an acknowledgement.

"Yeah, cuzz; I did nine months," I stated proudly.

"Let's walk around the corner to the liquor store and cop some crazy eight and smoke a fat one," Brown said smiling.

"Righteous, I'm down with that," I replied.

Gangster Brown introduced me to other Eight Treys while on our way to PJ's Liquor Store on Florence and Normandie. I met Devil, Harv Dogg, Trey Ball, Eight-Ball, Junebug, Clint, Bones, Crazy Dee, Vamp, and a youngster who could do more with a dirt bike than any white kid I knew. He could do block-long wheelies, jump over milk crates etc; he was only thirteen, but later would become a major factor in the Eight-Trey hood taking on the name Monster Kody. There were other notable ghetto stars in that area; Cutes, Rusty, Mousie, and Glen.

By noon, I had convinced my Mom her car needed washing. I volunteered to take it to the local drive thru car wash, a ploy to take it for a spin in my old neighborhood.

"Boy, you better hurry up and get back. Don't wreck my car either. I ain't playing with you," she responded as I stood there smiling from ear to ear like a Cheshire cat; my hand held out for the car keys.

Driving West up Florence Avenue to Crenshaw Boulevard, I made a left on 60th Street, stopping at Keniston Avenue.

I passed several car washes on the way. And didn't even think about stopping. Leaving the car running in the middle of the street, in park, I honked the horn, and said, "Get y'all's lazy asses up!" I shouted as I exited the bright yellow Dodge Duster.

Sheila was the first out of the door wearing a smile as bright as the afternoon sun. "Hey babes! How long you staying out this time?" Sheila joked.

Although pun was intended, I detected serious concern in the tone of her voice. We had been together off and on since she was thirteen years old. Unsure of how long I'd stay out of jail, Sheila found it wise to play our relationship one day at a time. We remained sexual companions and very good friends.

"C'm here and give me a hug, nigga," Sheila said as she put her arms around me.

"Damn you got buffed as hell! What they feeding you all in there?" she asked.

"It's what I wasn't getting baby, and that's sex!" I said slyly trying to put in my bid early.

"Hmmph," Sheila said approvingly, "I'll say."

"Can we get together sometime later, babes?" I asked with puppy dog eyes.

"I guess, come by tonight, and don't get lost over some bitch's house," Sheila said rocking back on her heels with her hands on her hips.

Sheila had fully developed since the last time we were together. She was dark chocolate with a slant in her eyes as if she were mixed with Black and Asian. She had long black hair, full Nubian lips, and a body at sixteen that would put any grown woman to shame. Sheila wanted me as bad as I wanted her. Women were always eager to get first dibs on a man fresh out of prison. They know the sex will be good!

"Where's your brother, girl?" I asked.

"You know that nigga ain't ever home. He lives in the streets!" Sheila answered, figuratively.

"What about Helen; where's she at?" I asked looking over her shoulder.

"Helen!" Sheila yelled at the top of her lungs.

"What bitch! Quit screaming my name," Helen yelled back from inside.

"C'm here, Helen," Sheila whined.

Damn, I wanted to say, as Big Helen appeared at the door, big as ever.

"Hey, Helen, look who's back," Sheila beamed proudly.

"Hey man; long time, no see," Helen said, maneuvering down the porch as quickly as her huge body could carry her, giving me a bear hug.

"You stay out of those places man. Ain't shit going on up in there," she said, with genuine concern.

"Helen, it ain't like I'm trying to go to jail."

"Well, I'm glad you're home anyway," Helen smiled.

"What they feeding ya'll in those places? Boy you have gotten so big," she added.

"Potatoes, potatoes and more potatoes. I'm sick of them," I replied, vowing never to eat another potato.

"Well, you look good, man," Helen said.

"Get off my man's jock," Sheila interrupted, with jealousy in her voice.

"Girl, pa-lease, James is like my little brother," Helen responded.

"N.E. Way, babes, I'll be back later, okay?" I said to Sheila, putting her on cue.

"Oh yeah, okay, see you later," Sheila caught on.

"Tell Billy to have his ass home tonight Helen, I'm anxious to see my homie."

"I'll make sure, hon. I know you two can't live without each other," she joked.

Helen was right. Every since Billy and I met we were like two peas in a pod. We were down with each other for whatever. We sexed females together on double dates in the back seats of g-rides and stole anything we could get our hands on, having even broken into a ghetto cleaners once stealing used clothes.

"Billy is my main man," I said to no one in particular.

As I thought about it, Billy would give me the shirt off his back if I needed it. A very unselfish homie with a good heart well liked among many. Billy Dee, the young ladies called the suave youngster after he got his hair processed, looking like Billy Dee Williams, the famed black actor.

We'd stay out all night sitting in g-rides on Keniston Avenue drinking Olde English 800 while listening to the radio consumed in our own thoughts. Billy would always fall asleep first.

"Pass the bottle homie," I'd say, waking Billy.

He'd wake up, take another swig on the bottle, passing it to me he'd say, "Kill it cuzz."

There is no homie in the world like him, I thought smiling.

As I pulled the Dodge Duster back into the driveway on Halldale

Avenue, I was met by my irate Mom.

"Boy, where you been all day with my car?" She asked.

"Mom, I told you that I was going to wash the car, dag!" I whined.

"Boy, that car looking like it ain't had a drop of water on it; give me my keys," she said becoming more agitated.

"Can't do nothing right boy, I'm telling you," blah, blah, blah, she went on as I handed her the keys, tuning her out.

I was thinking about my upcoming rendezvous with Sheila, damn that girl is thick, I thought and smiled. At about the same time the door bell rang.

"I'll get it," I shouted from the kitchen.

Opening the door, I recognized the face of Gangster Brown.

"What's up, cuzz?" Brown said smiling.

"Damn, homie, ever since I met you you've been smiling, what's so damn funny," I joked.

"That's cause I'm always on full homie, Crazy 800 and weed; I stay high nigga," Brown said without any reservation whatsoever.

"Right on homie, I feel you," I nodded.

"N.E. ways homie, I came over to tell you that Derexie wants to meet you."

"Derexie, who is she?" I asked.

"Your neighbor; she lives across the street," Brown pointed.

"Is that right?" I smiled.

"You mean the bow-legged cutie with the little gap between her front teeth?"

"Yeah, and she wants to meet you fool," Brown added, still smiling.

"You ain't got to say no more homie, I'm outta here. Talk to you later," I said, already halfway down the yard.

"A'ight homie," Brown said.

Derexie was a young lady who had a lot more class than the other girls in the neighborhood. She was a homebody. You could catch her home almost anytime, never in the streets. She was cocoa brown complexioned, slightly freckled smooth face. The early evening chat with my new neighbor consisted of us getting to know each other.

"I helped your Mom move into her house, she's really nice. I never knew she had a son," Derexie said.

"Thanks for helping her. That was good looking out," I said.

"I wanted to meet you when I found out you were her son," she said bashfully.

"By the way, my name is Derexie," she formally introduced herself.

"Pleasure to meet you, Derexie," I greeted back with a Kodak smile.

"I'm James."

"Would you like a glass of water or juice?" she asked in an attempt to fill the void in the conversation.

"Yeah, sure; I'll take a glass please."

"Which one?" she asked on her way to the icebox.

"Excuse me?" I answered, realizing I had not heard the question, having been distracted by her brown skin thighs that were exposed by cut-off jeans.

"Water or juice?" she posed the question again, mentally taking note of what caused the distraction.

"Juice please," I said, all the while kicking myself in the ass for allowing the female to see I was so easily enticed by the game she inadvertently played.

A woman, no matter what age, wants a challenge. Any game she sees as easy to play is no game she wants to be part of.

"Would you like to listen to some music?" Derexie asked.

"You got the Isley's?"

"Their latest album, *Voyage to Atlantis?*" she inquired.

"Yeah, that be jamming," I smiled.

"Righteous," she agreed.

After a few hours in the company of the curious neighbor, I retreated with my head in the clouds and relaxed. So much running around in one day had prematurely exhausted me. I thought about Derexie and how she would make a decent girlfriend. Not trying to make a move during the first encounter was always a sign of self control in the eyes of any woman. If a woman wanted you and the time was right she'd let you know.

Suddenly it came as an afterthought. Damn, I gotta go see my boy Billy. He should have gotten word by now that I'm out. I contemplated going back into the streets when a voice shook me out of my thoughts.

"Yeah, Mom," I answered.

"Pick up the phone; it's Sheila,"Mom yelled from the bedroom.

Oh, man! Damn near forgot about our little date tonight. She's gonna be straight tripping. I looked at the clock on the dresser noticing I had spent more time than I realized at Derexie's.

"Okay, mom; you can hang the phone up now. I got it!"

"Hello, Sheila?"

"Yeah." she answered.

"I was just thinking about you."

"Billy's dead," Sheila said softly.

"Stop playing, girl," I said, thinking that Billy was on the other line.

All I heard were muffled sounds and sobs. Quite obvious Sheila was crying. In all the time I've known Sheila, I've never known her to cry.

"I'm on my way over now," I said in a monotone voice, as if I just entered the twilight zone.

As I reached Keniston Avenue, there was an unusual activity of folks pulling on and off the block. Everyone was over to the Smith's to find out what had happened to Billy Dee, and to pay condolences.

The official account was that Billy and two others held up an all-night Lerner's gas station on 79th and Crenshaw Boulevard.

Billy, .45 automatic in hand, stood over the manager getting money from the floor safe. The robbery was quickly foiled when Los Angeles police, 77th Street Division, converged on the scene unnoticed.

Billy, not wanting to do a day in jail, fled on foot when police ordered him to drop his weapon.

Sprinting towards a brick wall that would separate him from overzealous police officers, Billy made it to the top but was felled by a blast to the base of his neck by a police pump shotgun.

Billy Smith, the ladies' man, stick-up kid, greatest homeboy in the world, died within minutes at a very young age sprawled out on the pavement of the gas station lot.

The funeral was held in a medium size church on 39th and Denker Avenue. Many had come to pay their respects to the youngster so many loved. The church was filled to the capacity. There were so many mourners, folks stood outside just to be able to say their last goodbye.

Crips from all over attended, as did Bloods, hustlers, players, and a host of relatives. *"Be Ever Wonderful"* by Earth, Wind & Fire played softly through the funeral procession eliciting cries from grandmother's, babies, and young women. Men shed angry tears for their fallen homie. Billy's death was a stark reminder of how the streets could just snatch life away in the blink of an eye. Yet life went on, the cycle of madness continued in urban cities of America.

◆ ◆ ◆

During the summer of 1977, I met Stanley Tookie Williams. Tookie was an original Westside Crip who rose quickly through the ranks eventually becoming a leader. He ruled the Westside through intimidation, physical force and fear.

Big Tookie lived on 69th Street between Denker Avenue and Western. I lived around the corner on 70th Street between Halldale and

Denker Avenue. Some of the Crips in that area who were Eight Trey Gangsters would go over Tookie's to lift weights. There was Eight Ball, Monster Kody, his brother Kerwin, G.C. and Blair. They invited me to come with them to lift weights there.

Tookie's living room was filled with weights and dumbbells. There were several arm benches, two bench press stations, a preacher bench and squat rack. Homies lifted iron fervently to the sounds of James Brown's *"Big Payback"* and *"Body Heat"*. Parliment Funkadelic and Barry White also blasted over house speakers.

Only chosen homies were allowed to hang around, play dozens or lift weights without being subjected to ridicule or a beat down. Other regulars there were; Big Jackie from Compton (Tookie's best friend) and Gimel Barnes (founder of Avalon Garden Crips). Between Tookie and Gimel you could not tell who was bigger, both of them measured twenty three inch arms. Tookie looked like a big black shiny Buddha, Gimel was yellow complexioned and kept his hair corn-rolled.

There was also Big Mansion, an aspiring boxer who was Tookie's sidekick and Tookie's Step Brother, then known as Lil Tookie.

A few weeks after I started lifting weights there, Tookie and Gimel got into a dispute over some issue almost coming to blows, until Jackie intervened. Gimel stormed out cursing, vowing never to return.

Tookie, Gimel and Jackie were a three man team. Now they needed another third man. Jackie asked me to stand in for Gimel Barnes. I told

Jackie that I could not hit the heavy iron they were lifting. Tookie and Gimel both had over five hundred pounds bench press, back arming over two hundred for reps. He responded telling me just do what you can do, no one is expecting you to do more. So, I was in. I was honored to be able to be on Big Took's workout team.

Our workout sessions started Monday thru Friday at 3:00p.m. ending somewhere around 6:00p.m. After a grueling workout we'd re-energize making homemade protein drinks, a mixture of; Egg white powder, Brewer's Yeast, Wheat Germ, Enfamil (yes, Enfamil, a high protein content), and amino acids. We would put everything into a blender, mix and drink.

I packed on muscle quickly. I became a student of the Crip leader in areas of weight lifting and character as I got to know Tookie on a personal level. Tookie, Jackie and I worked out together over a year.

The year of 1978 was much the same, fun under the California sun. Heatwave, Slave, Marvin Gaye and Cameo's funky beats played at Los Angeles' night clubs; The Workshop (formerly called Carwash), Showcase, Carolina West and Blueberry Hill.

Tookie worked as a bouncer in at least three of these dance clubs. I would get a free pass through whichever door he worked, the dance floor would be packed with youngsters from all over Los Angeles, Watts, Compton and Long Beach. Angel Dust (mint leaves sprayed with PCP), was very popular among partiers in this era and would be smoked in a thin joint.

Partiers experienced euphoria dancing until daybreak, leaving the club in a stupor or in the company of someone they hadn't come with.

Eventually Tookie and I smoked Angel Dust, then Sherm sticks (Sherman cigarette dipped in PCP). Ironically, we smoked after a workout. Initially, smoking Sherm did not hinder my workouts. But, Tookie had access to an unlimited supply. He, along with me, would simply strong arm local dealers whenever we wanted more. Soon it was a daily ritual. I could barely recuperate from the last high before Tookie would be at my door again, with a freshly dipped wet stick.

Clearly, it did not seem to affect him at all. My zombied out mind was screaming for help. I had to shake Tookie like a wet suit.

Tookie is a legend, and someone I always looked up to. However, he was falling behind what L.A.'s fast lane dictated.

I was lured by the need to catch up with rising ghetto stars who were making fast money and splurging with fast women. I started jacking with the local Eight Trey's.

"Hanging out in the hood like mascots ain't putting no scrilla in our pockets," I convinced Clint, Junebug and Gangster Brown.

Thus elaborate robberies were planned. We combed the County of Los Angeles looking for establishments that were close to the freeway that would enable us in escaping the area quickly.

Chapter 6 211 with a Vengeance

Most supermarkets left back door ramps unattended during the wee hours of the night so that produce delivery trucks could unload crates of fresh fruits and vegetables. However, it was a major security breach, allowing a intruder easy access into the supermarket unnoticed.

Three of us sat in the parking lot in a stolen Chevy Camaro, watching and waiting. The dock workers seemed to be consumed in their work, unaware they were being clocked. I was the first to speak, breaking the deadly silence, "They're done unloading now. As soon as that truck pulls out let's go in."

Inside the manager made his rounds. "Marge, did you take all of today's receipts upstairs?"

"We need to get everything ready, Brinks will be here shortly," Dave said with a weary expression.

"All of the receipts have been sent upstairs over an hour ago Dave, Mary is bagging the money now," Marge answered.

Dave's weary expression turned into a smile, "Thanks, Marge."

Dave Dixon had been the manager at the Safeway market just over a month. He had recently been promoted and was on pins and needles every since. It was still a probation period for him.

The Burgundy Camaro pulled into the ramp area at the back of the supermarket.

"No one is on to us, put your faces on," I said referring to the blue face ski mask.

Exiting the Camaro each man was consumed in his own thoughts. No matter how intricate the planning, one could not control the outcome. The power the robber gets is addicting, the spoils are incentives to repeat it over and over.

Keeping our weapons sealed we entered the building. In all her years at the inner city Safeway market Marge had never experienced being robbed. When she saw the two masked bandits she was taken aback.

"Come with us," I said, the shotgun doing all of the necessary intimidating.

One of us lagged behind on the back dock as a measure to keep security on that particular area.

"Don't worry ma'am, this is a robbery. We're not here to hurt anyone," I said.

"Are you the manager?" I asked.

"No, I'm the assistant manager," she answered, barely audible.

The manager did not bother to look through the peep hole when he heard the knock on the door. He hadn't expected it to be anyone other than Marge with Brinks armored security to pick up the money from the safe. When Dave opened the door he was overwhelmed by shotgun wielding robbers. Marge, and the store clerks were with them.

"Get that safe open!" the man with a pistol barked.

Brinks truck pulled up at the front entrance of the supermarket as scheduled.

"Hey Joe, last pickup isn't it?"

"Yeah, Charlie. After this we're back to the station, a night's work done."

"Good God man, I'm beat," Charlie said, "This new allergy medication is really draining me."

Taking their weapons out of their holsters as company policy dictates to ward off robbery attempts, they headed inside. Brinks drivers were given keys to the stores they made pickups so they would not be standing around waiting for entry like sitting ducks.

Unfortunately, Brinks routine had been compromised.

Walking upstairs security knocked on the door causing it to come slightly ajar. Pushing it open they noticed store employees lying all over the floor bound with duct tape and gagged. Safe wide open.

At the same time Brinks guards discovered the employees, we had just finished loading the last bag of money into the trunk of a late model Ford, the switch car, blocks away. We were now at a comfortable distance on the freeway, safe and sound.

The fact that the robbery had been committed one block from 77th Street Police Station stunned robbery-homicide detectives. Even more, the arrogance of the robbers leaving a scrawled message inside the empty safe. It read Billy Dee, Rest in Peace.

"Who is Billy Dee," the younger detective inquired, dusting the safe for prints.

"The Smith kid taken down during a gas station hold up last year on Crenshaw Boulevard," his partner seethed.

"Some dipshit has a hair up his ass about the killing. I would like to catch the bastard while he has his nose in some safe," he added.

We enjoyed the exploits from the heist celebrating like ghetto stars. I pulled my brand new Sedan de Ville onto the front lawn to prevent some thief from stealing the car.

"Boy, whose car is that you're driving?" my mother yelled from behind the screen door.

"Damn, I knew it," I mumbled under my breath. I had expected to be bombarded with a zillion questions, having no logical answers.

"It's my friend's car, momma. He let me use it," I answered, thinking of nothing else that made any sense.

It's unusual that an eighteen year old, who doesn't even have a job, be able to afford such luxury.

I stood outside admiring the Cadillac's shiny, glistening chrome rims beam against the sun's ray, feeling proud that I had a heap of money. I beamed from inside out.

Before I could make it back inside, I was confronted by Mom.

"Boy, I don't know what is going on? But, nobody in their right mind is going to let you drive their brand new car and you don't even have a license. I'm not trying to hear that nonsense. You take that car and get it out of my yard, right now!"

The writing was on the wall. It was my out, so to say. I was eighteen years old. I lived under my mother's roof long enough, particularly when I was causing my mother nothing but headaches. It was time for me to move on and take care of my own responsibilities.

I started the car, backing it out the yard. I didn't know where I would be going or for what purpose. Inserting a cassette into the tape deck, The Whispers crooned *"Olivia"*. A song about a woman turned out by a wolf in lambs clothing; a metaphoric melody indicating how smooth talking players manipulate vulnerable minded females.

Cruising down Normandie Avenue while listening to the sweet

sounds of music, I relaxed. With my split of cash, I could live comfortably until I could find a small apartment to rent. I made a mental note to search for one the next morning.

As the Sedan de Ville eased through traffic, I signaled a left turn at Venice and Normandie Avenue heading west towards the Wilshire District, for no apparent reason other than cruising. The sedan crawled a couple blocks as I watched the ladies file out of their offices during the noon hour. It was there that I saw her. She was deep chocolate and stacked in all the right places.

"Damn, baby. Is all of that you?" Or is my mind playing tricks on me?" I grinned a devilish smile.

"You got too much booty girl! Can I holla at you?" I pitched, hanging my head out the car window.

"I ain't got time right now baby," she said in a tone that commanded respect from foul mouth men. I need to bring him down off his high horse. He's just too loose with his lips. But, damn, he got it going on. A little young, but that's cool too. She thought.

"Let me get your digits then. I'm patient," I offered.

"Your mouth is too foul, which implies you don't know how to respect a woman," she said, stopping in mid stride, putting her hands on her hips.

"That may be true," I cleverly interjected, sidetracking a

confrontation that would get me nowhere. "But, I promise you I can be trained. Besides, there's a little dog in every man," I laughed.

"You so silly," she laughed back.

The woman had finally dropped her guard. It was an encore performance. I turned a potential rejection around by making fun of it. Humor has always been the best way to a woman's heart. Besides money. I had allowed my sensitive side to reveal itself in an attempt to get what I wanted.

"Well, I guess you can call me if you tone down some of your sexual overtones. I'm a woman, not some sex object. "Whatever you say, your highness," I cheesed.

"Whose new car are you driving?"

"Anyway, you better take it back before you get a ticket," she joked.

"This is my new car, baby," I beamed.

"Hmmph! Where do you work to be able to afford such luxuries?" she quizzed.

Looking up and down the block I motioned with my hand. "I work these streets baby."

"I'll say," she gestured her shoulders up then down.

"Can I give you a ride home?"

"Sure, why not," she answered.

She was twenty three years old and recently moved from Chicago to live with her older sister. As I pulled up alongside this woman in my brand new Cadillac I looked like the opportunity she had secretly been waiting for. In her eyes, I was money and money was a sign of security. An element she lacked in her life.

Sliding into the Sedan de Ville, she slumped down in the velour cushioned seat, exhausted. It was like night and day compared to the city bus she had been getting around on.

The scuffling, jockeying for seats and being short on change was mentally draining.

"This sure is nice," she smiled inwardly.

"Thanks," I said, leaning extra hard.

I popped in a tape by a group called, The Jazz Crusaders. The song was "*Street Life*". We rode in silence savoring the moment.

"You can make a left here, then slow down when you get to the middle of the block, I stay in the yellow condo on the left."

"Should I park?" I asked slyly.

"You can drop me off here, I'm a big girl. Besides, I don't date the first day I meet someone. It's really not appropriate. So call me tonight, cool? Here's my number," she said.

"Who should I ask for?"

"Excuse me?"

"You didn't tell me your name," I said.

"Oh, I'm sorry. I'm Chiquita."

"Your name is?"

"James Lacy," I answered.

"Have a nice day and drive safe," she said.

"You too," I said my eyes never leaving her body as she walked towards the condo. I barely heard the cars honk behind me.

"Yeah, yeah, okay! I'll be out your way in a minute," I mumbled under my breath while mentally taking pictures of the chocolate star.

She turned around extending her thumb and pinkie finger, a gesture as if she were holding a phone to her ear.

"Call me," Her mouth formed without words actually coming out.

Chiquita, although she did not date on her first day, soon fell for me. Eventually we found a place and moved in together, enjoying a romantic lifestyle. She would be the first woman I tried a serious monogamous relationship with.

The relationship was so fulfilling it seemed as if we were destined for one another. But, when a man does not have a plan, his future is subject to failure. There is also a verse in the Bible that reads; "A fool and his money will soon part". I was supporting my means through robberies. Time after time, I put myself at risk during each heist.

It was the robbery of Boy's supermarket on Jefferson and Western Avenue that careened my criminal career, brushing me with a stroke of ill fated destiny. Without any planning whatsoever, my partner in crime and I concocted a fly by night scheme.

"Go into the store first," I said to my partner.

"Draw suspicion to the security guard by looking sneaky as if you are shoplifting. When he follows you down the aisle, I'll draw down on him from behind. We take his weapon which gives us control of the store and safe."

There was one major drawback, the market was full of evening shoppers and it was in the hood. Hood victims of crime and suburban victims do not necessarily respond the same. Hood victims either have nothing or everything to lose, it's all the same.

My partner in crime and I entered the market concealing a sawed off shotgun. The security guard as expected followed my partner down the aisle. We immediately sandwiched him. I commanded the security guard to put his hands up where I could see them. The guard who was armed with a .357 magnum in his hip holster just stood there and stared at me, foolishly disobeying the command. Seconds ticked as we squared off with each other.

Damn, I thought. I hope this fool is not contemplating on becoming a hero. A million thoughts raced through my mind in a matter of seconds. I just could not understand why he would not comply. Is he deaf? I thought. Not allowing another second to go by so that the guard could build his courage, I barked louder, "Get your muther freakin hands up!"

I felt my fingers tighten around the butt of the shotgun, my palms moisten. The last thing a professional bandit wants to do is commit murder. He would rather abort the robbery than to kill. Generally, he is there for the money. This is why planning, timing and sophistication facilitates a smooth take. It's the difference between finesse and savagery.

There are more desperate robbers these days. The desperate robber and their rash acts have caused the professional to realize that crime does not pay.

The security guard shot his hands up, my partner disarmed him. With the security guards gun in our possession I quickly handcuffed him and marched him to the front of the market. However, while going through the charades with the security guard everyone had slipped out the market, even the store manager who had the keys to the safe. Realizing the robbery had been foiled, we fled also, leaving the guard handcuffed but unharmed.

Less than a week later, my friend Adrienne asked me for a ride to her

Long Beach apartment. It was 2:00 a.m., we were driving east down Florence Avenue towards Figueroa. Just before turning onto the Harbor freeway, 77th Street police division stopped the Cadillac allegedly for a traffic violation.

"Pull over your vehicle," the officer announced over the bull horn. Red and blue police lights flickered wildly as the officers approached the Cadillac with caution.

"I need to see your driver's license," the senior officer said with an attitude.

"I must have left it in my other pants pocket," I lied quickly.

"Would you step out the vehicle, Sir," he said with authority.

As I stood on the curb the officer began a field interrogation asking questions, Adrienne still sitting in the passenger seat.

"Where were you all headed to?"

"What's his name?"

"What's her name?"

When it was apparent that our stories coincided, he probed deeper. "Is it okay if I search your vehicle?" he asked.

It was common knowledge among criminals that you did not have to give police permission to search your vehicle. They had to have probable cause.

"No Sir, you cannot," I answered, knowing I had guns in my trunk.

Frustrated that I had not given him permission he scrutinized the inside of the Caddie from the outside. The officer spotted the butt of a toy gun sticking out from under the passenger's seat, so he claimed. This gave the overzealous officer reasonable suspicion to search based on presumption the gun was real.

During the search, the officer noticed a plastic baggie protruding from Adrienne's purse. Inside was an ounce of marijuana. It was enough to impound the vehicle as well as arrest the both of us.

At the substation Adrienne quickly confessed to the marijuana leaving me only with a traffic violation. The traffic violation held me long enough while the police impound meticulously searched the Cadillac. I had foolishly rode dirty with the .357 magnum that had been taken from the security guard at the Boy's supermarket, a shotgun, ski masks, duffel bags and gloves. All tools of the trade.

After the discovery of these items in the trunk of my car, robbery investigators put a no bail hold on me. As expected, the .357 magnum was traced back to the market robbery. Investigators conducted a photo lineup with the security guard and I was quickly identified as one of the robbers who held him at gun point taking his weapon.

My photo was taken to other establishments where similar robberies were reported. A total of six armed robberies had been directly linked to me. I was indicted and formally charged. Then transported to the Los Angeles County Jail. I had barely turned nineteen.

Chapter 7 Flashlight Therapy

The Los Angeles County Jail in 1979 was a den of violence. There were robberies, rapes, mayhem and murder occurring on a daily basis. The city's toughest gangs roamed the jail quarters.

Weaker inmates were preyed upon so viciously that one of the quarters had been cleared out and it had been designated as a "softie" tank. Mainly inexperienced white suburban youth who had fear written all over their faces were held there. These were the ones usually spotted by seasoned predators.

The deputies who patrolled the county jail were corn fed white men who were recruited from southern states; Georgia, Mississippi and Louisiana. Most of them had racist overtones and a propensity for violence. They would not hesitate to crack your head with the flashlight they carried. Convicts and Deputies generally referred to these beatings as a dose of "Flashlight Therapy".

"Don't get out of line with these deputies youngster, they will kill you here," some of the older cons warned me.

Los Angeles County Jail had a notorious reputation for inmate fatalities at the hands of Sheriff Deputies. It was common knowledge among prisoners and regular citizens alike.

In the 9500 module there are endless rows of bunk beds. However, prisoners were not designated to specific bunks.

Prisoners were booked in throughout the night and had to make their own sleeping arrangements provided a bed was available. Cliques laid claim to every bed in the dorm, so it were the cliques, who controlled who slept where. If you were not affiliated with a gang, or did not know someone, you were going to be sleeping on the floor unless you paid for a bunk.

The average stay in 9500 was seven days. Prisoners waited there to be classified. Classification is a process that determines which module the prisoner will be housed in. Gambling, fighting, rapping, smoking and excessive chatter went on throughout the night in 9500 dorm keeping sleep deprived prisoners awake. A blaring P.A. system announced prisoner's names for court line every morning at 2:00 a.m. It almost reminded one of being in a New York City subway with all of the activity going on.

Young thugs patrolled the dorm preying on victims for cash. At Los Angeles County Jail, prisoners could receive forty dollars each visiting day. Since there was no record how many times a prisoner received cash on visits, it was not uncommon for prisoners to have enough cash to secure their own bail while being housed there.

I befriended Tiger, from Watts, who was holding down a section for incoming Crips. We were a mischief group. Always on the prowl for a come up. So when we saw the two white prisoners casually walking through the dorm carrying money pouches on a string tied around their necks they seemed like easy marks.

"How much you think they got in them pouches?" Tiger asked me.

"I don't know homie, but the pouches sure look fat," I said while scrutinizing the awkward pair.

Approaching the two whites we snatched money pouches from the both of them.

"Let me get this up off you fool."

The frightened pair darted directly towards the deputies' booth shouting, "Help! Help!"

I could not believe my eyes and ears. Unnoticed, I made my way to the bunk beds, laid down on one of them and pretended to be sleep. As the deputies came out of the Plexiglas enclosed booth, I could hear the two white prisoners identifying Tiger, who had been standing nearby looking dumbfounded.

"That's one of them right there," I heard one say.

The pair led deputies down the aisle to the bunk where I was.

"Hey get your ass up!" the deputy ordered shining his flashlight on me.

I laid there a couple seconds thinking he would go away for some odd reason.

"If I have to tell you one more time, I'm kicking your black ass!" he angrily warned me.

Using better judgment, I got up rubbing my eyes.

"What's going on man?" I asked playing possum.

As I followed the deputy out of the module into the hallway, I noticed Tiger standing with his hands behind his back, handcuffed, nose on the wall.

"Take these two dip shits to the hole," the sergeant standing nearby demanded.

The deputies escorted us up a set of escalators, down a corridor, then down another set of escalators.

It's easy to get lost in here was all I seemed to be thinking. We reached the module euphemistically known as the "hole". Speaking through the intercom, the deputy requested entry inside the isolation quarters.

"I have two prisoners for security housing," he said.

Buzzzzz, clank! The steel door opened, then closed back behind us once we entered.

"What are their charges," the senior officer over the security housing module asked.

"Strong armed robbery," the escorting deputies said.

"Take one of them to Charlie range and put the other on Able range. Change them into jumpsuits," the senior officer said appearing to be busy with some paperwork.

On the right hand side of the front entrance was a dingy elevator that was used to take me to the second level, Charlie range.

Two deputies escorting me ordered me to strip naked so that they could search me. This was standard procedure.

I stripped and stood there thinking; these fags are always looking in someone's ass. I felt awkward, my bare feet getting cold from the dirty concrete floor. One of the deputies began to ask questions.

"Are you a Crip?"

I had been wearing blue Reebok tennis shoes.

"Crips wear blue," he remarked.

"What neighborhood do you live in?" inquired the other.

"I live in Riverside," I lied quickly sidetracking any gang affiliations. I knew it was a non combat zone at that time.

"Don't Crips hang out there?" he pried further.

"Not that I know of," I answered.

"If you're not a gangbanger then why do you wear your hair corn-rolled?" the shorter deputy asked; he resembled a human rodent.

Because my hair is long, idiot, I wanted to say. But seeing I was being baited into a trap, I shut down answering any further questions for fear I might snap and say something I may regret.

Seeing the frustration in my body language, the deputies poked a little harder, asking one question after another as I stood there buck naked.

"Hey asshole, I asked you a question," the human rodent shouted.

"I did not hear you man," I responded trying to conceal the anger in my voice.

"Turn around and face the wall," the taller deputy ordered.

Completely naked I faced the wall. I was thinking how much I hated authority because of the vulnerable position I found myself in, when all of a sudden I felt my body being jerked back by human rodent who had his arms around my neck trying to put me in a choke hold.

As I was pulled down, I felt short rabbit punches to my ribs. Initially, the punches didn't faze me. I'm thinking it was just another rough up by soft ass cops.

"This shit ain't even fazing me," I wanted to say aloud to tick them off even more.

As I was thrown to the floor the seriousness of the matter began to unfold, the taller deputy now involved began kicking my naked body while human rodent pulled out his flashlight beating my back and shoulders.

I curled into a fetal position protecting my head and face. I overheard the county jail paging system.

"Code 415, officers need assistance, 2200 module." I realized it was me they were referring to. By now boot kicks, punches and flashlights seemed to be coming from all directions, I could no longer fend off blows.

One deputy banged my head with his long steel flashlight like a kid trying to break open a pinata at a backyard birthday party.

Up until that point I had been holding it all in, not wanting the deputies to see they were hurting me. I did so out of pride, yet the pain was so unbearable I couldn't withstand it any longer.

As I lay there being beaten, I'm thinking I don't want to die like this on the dirty floor. I think of fatalities I've heard about at the Los Angeles County jail from the hands of the deputies and cannot help but think my life will end the same way.

These fools are trying to kill me, I realized.

"AAAAAAHHHHHHH! AAAAAARRRRRRRRHHHHHHH!" I screamed in agony. My voice hadn't even sounded like my own. The death scream carried through the segregation unit which probably saved me from a fatal beating.

The deputies finally stopped. I no longer felt the blows. I propped up on one hand finding myself surrounded by ten or more blood thirsty deputies. I bled profusely from my scalp and my shoulders were bruised.

A burly, white haired, red faced sergeant with a barrel belly protruding from his waistline wobbled through the pack of deputies.

"Get up off my floor, you're getting blood on it," he said.

I started to get up but my leg gave out from under me. Although it had feeling, it would not take my own weight.

Tears of anger welled up in my eyes, but I dare not shed one. I had just experienced racism and brutality at its worst. Ain't this a bitch, I thought.

"Get up, I say!" the sergeant yelled, his voice laced with hatred and indignation.

Repulsed at the insensitive treatment of someone who was supposed to maintain discipline in the ranks of the deputies and unable to control my composure any longer, I shouted back, "I can't you fat bastard! My leg, I think it's broke."

The sergeant turned beet red ordering someone to call for medical assistance while I still lay on the dirty, cold pavement with a wounded leg and ego.

It was a nightmare. How did I ever get caught up in this? I forgot so quickly. The medics arrived and a nurse rolled in a wheelchair beside me.

"Get in this chair," barrel belly said.

"I can't," I stated. "If I could I would not be lying here," I spoke in the nastiest tone I could utter.

The deputies grabbed my naked body, plopping me into the wheelchair.

"Where-are-your-clothes?" the nurse who was a foreigner asked speaking broken English.

"I-don't-know-where-they-are," I mimicked the nurse sarcastically.

"Get him a blanket" barrel belly interrupted, as he barked orders to one of the deputies.

I was then escorted down the escalators to the infirmary on the first floor to receive medical treatment. Due to the trauma from the "flashlight therapy" a tendon in my left leg had been ruptured. I had two small gashes in my scalp that required six or seven stitches respectively. The corn-row braids I wore acted as a cushion from the blows to my scalp. It could have been much worse. I also had heavy bruising on my shoulders and back.

I was assigned to the medical unit two days, locked down twenty four seven, when a Deputy Ashford, who had been working the hospital wing doing overtime, stopped at my door.

"Hey Lacy, you are definitely a survivor man."

I gave him a confused look.

"I was one of the deputies who responded to Code Four Fifteen the other day. You took one hell of a beating."

I could not help wondering how many licks he himself got in on me. But at the same time I believed he was trying to tell me something.

That night I wrote a letter to my friend, Wanda, detailing the incident. After that letter was mailed, I was held incommunicado.

Wanda, who tried to visit me to gather facts about the incident was always given various reasons why she could not visit. For example; Deputies telling her that I was at court that day, had been transferred to another jail, or that I was not in their custody.

Wanda began making calls to persons of authority. It was through her persistence that a formal in-house inquiry was conducted by a high ranking jail commander. Due to concerns of safety, but more less a retaliatory move, I was moved to module 1750 also known as "Highpower". This module, a high security lock up unit, consisted of single cells. In Highpower, prisoners come out their cells in waist and leg shackles. There is a booth with a one way mirror that runs along the length of the tier in front of the open cell bars giving deputies access at viewing prisoners at all times.

Among some of the infamous prisoners or notable celebrity prisoners housed in Highpower at one time or another were; Charles Manson, Richard (Night Stalker) Ramirez, Kenneth (Freeway Killer) Bianchi, O.J. Simpson, Todd (Child Actor) Bridges and the Menendez brothers. I was held there for a few weeks for my own protection, during the investigation of the jail house beating.

Five months later, I pled out to six counts of armed robbery. The State of California offered me a plea bargain, a minimum of eight years on each count to run concurrent with each other.

With an eight year plea, I would serve no more than five years, actual time. Considering all of the robberies that had been committed this was considered a sweetheart deal.

I also asked my attorney to submit a request to the judge asking that Chiquita and I be married after sentencing.

I suddenly came to the realization that having a wife in my corner while doing time would be very beneficial. The Department of Corrections had conjugal visits (trailer visits), on the weekend every ninety days. Provided that a convict was legally married.

Ten days after getting sentenced and married I caught the chain to go serve out my time. I was twenty years old. It would start my tumultuous career as a criminal offender.

Chapter 8 California State Prison

The Grey Goose's first stop would be California Institution for Men in Chino, California, commonly referred to as Chino. Chino has a reception center for prisoners newly admitted into the Department of Corrections. At the reception center prisoners are diagnosed and see a guidance counselor to determine which of several California prison facilities they will be housed at. The average stay at the reception center is six to eight weeks.

Cells are racially segregated. Blacks cell with blacks, Whites with whites, Chicanos with one another. No one clique maintains any real control because of the short amount of time spent in Chino. However, as in any prison setting, tempers flare and situations get out of control between rival gangs from time to time. Racism in the California prison system is the norm and permeates its pores.

I was housed in Sycamore Unit at the reception facility. After seeing a guidance counselor, I was recommended to be designated to California Men's Colony(CMC), in San Luis Obisbo. CMC, was a resort style facility that offered a variety of vocational and educational programs. Prisoners had keys to their rooms. The reception center administrator was very selective who was designated to CMC because of the very lax environment. Prisoner's files were carefully screened; first termers with no bad conduct reports were selected.

"I'm putting you in for CMC," the guidance counselor informed me.

"I see this is your first term and you have no history of violence," he added.

"Thanks," I said. I knew that CMC was one of the best prisons in the state of California.

"Don't get your hopes too high; it's only a recommendation at this point."

"Any questions?" he asked, closing my brand new file.

"Nah," I answered.

Within a couple weeks after seeing the guidance counselor there was a cell house disturbance. Prisoners clogged their toilets causing them to stop up, flooding the tiers. We also burned paper and other debris throwing it out the cell onto the tier. The unit officers yelled through the bullhorn ordering us to stop, but we defiantly shook our cell bars screaming, "No! No! No! No!"

I was housed in the second cell from the front grill gate. As the guard stood there ordering us to stop he could see the different cells that were flooding and burning paper. He wrote those cell numbers down.

After the flooding and burning, the tactical squad assembled. They marched down the tiers stopping at the cells that were on the list. My cell was one of them.

"Back up to the bars and put your hands behind your back!" the tactical squad ordered, wearing full riot gear as a protective measure.

"You're not so bad now, are you?"

We knew it was better to be safe than sorry. Only a few distant obscenities were heard as fires smoldered. Some of the recalcitrant groups of prisoners were taken to the hole. I was taken also. While there, the guidance counselor came to my cell to see me. Upon my initial orientation he perceived me as someone who could be rehabilitated.

"You messed up your opportunity for the transfer to CMC by being involved in the disturbance last week, Lacy," Mr. Lambert expressed, shaking his head in disappointment.

"The program administrator is re-designating you to Duel Vocational Institution," he informed me.

The prison I was reassigned to was also known as "Gladiator School". It was in the city of Tracy, California. Staff as well as prisoners referred to the institution as Tracy or Gladiator School. The average age of prisoner in Tracy was between the ages of seventeen and thirty five years old. Tracy housed a lot of Youth Authority commitments who were unmanageable and who would not conform.

Tracy Prison was called Gladiator School because of the brawls that were frequently fought there.

Although there was a lot of knife play at Tracy only a couple killings occurred there over several years. No one really playing for keeps. But there were several racial attacks and retaliatory attacks that would keep the prison locked down anywhere from one month to six months at any given time.

When I entered Tracy the prison was on lock down status because of a previous racial brawl. The Southern California Mexicans were at war with Northern California Mexicans and African American prisoners. Aryans sided with the Southern California Mexicans in this ongoing war. New arrivals were afforded the privilege of coming out of their cell for tier time since they hadn't been at the institution when the past incident occurred. Six of us blacks were let out the first day with six Mexicans. All went well the first day.

After lock up, a tier orderly calling himself Seabisquit, from the Bay area, pushed up on my door.

"Hey, my man. The Mexicans are up to something. I think they are planning a move on the Blacks, watch your back. I have a metal fork, break the end off and sharpen it. It will make a good shank," Seabisquit whispered.

I had no understanding at that time of prison politics or guerilla warfare. The impression I got was that Seabisquit was attempting to use me as a pawn in whatever conflict had been going on before I arrived.

"No man, I'm cool on that. I just want to do my time and get out," I firmly replied.

"Fine with me brother," Seabisquit said as if he never made the pitch and kept it moving.

I thought that as long as I did not directly involve myself with prison politics I could stay clear of trouble. How wrong I was. I would soon learned that in the California prison system just skin color alone could be the determining factor between living and dying. No one was exempt.

The next day the same group of prisoners came out for tier time. It was Saturday. The Blacks were watching Soul Train in the dayroom. The Mexicans were on the tiers lying low for any stragglers. Suddenly, without warning, a young black darted through the doors of the dayroom sliding across the waxed floor in his cheaply manufactured tennis shoes.

"Hey man! Red just got moved on," the youngster said while trying to catch his breath.

Red, also a new arrival, had wandered up on the third tier by himself. The Mexicans seizing an opportunity for retaliation stabbed Red. It was all the group of us needed to hear as we jumped into action. Running onto the tier, we were met by Mexicans wielding makeshift weapons.

Apprehensive about a counter attack without weaponry, we faced them down, not breaking our ranks, looking for a weak point. I guess you can say that it was a Mexican standoff.

"Come on eh!" they baited us.

Fearing the Mexicans would find the courage they needed to attack us, I grabbed a empty fifty gallon steel barrel that was at arm's reach, tossing it, keeping them at bay. Around the same time, the goon squad rushed in carrying Big Bertha, the double barrel bean bag capable of knocking a prisoner off his feet temporarily disabling him.

"Up against the wall!" the goon squad shouted at us.

The Mexicans discarded their weapons. Everyone found a spot on the wall, hands up. The guards did a mandatory hand and torso check to see if anyone had acquired wounds during the altercation. A Mexican who had been less fortunate in getting rid of his weapon was quickly handcuffed and escorted to segregation. Red, who had been wounded was taken to segregation, I had a small cut on my finger from picking up the steel drum so was also taken to segregation (K-Wing).

Two weeks later I appeared before the segregation Lieutenant, after fabricating a story about me cutting my finger while trying to turn the broken channel knob on the television in the day room, I was released back to general population. My conduct towards conforming in prison drastically changed after realizing anything was subject to change at any time. I felt uncomfortable in the prison environment where environment was in control rather than man.

Upon my return to D-Unit my aggressive behavior towards authority increased drastically. I committed a series of six frivolous infractions in eight days. I received bad conduct reports for disobeying a direct order from a staff member, being late for work assignment, stealing fruit and sandwiches out of the prison dining room, blocking the window of my cell door with cardboard and other bad conduct reports.

"You have acquired several incident reports in a matter of days," one of the committee members said addressing me at a hearing.

"Your classification points have also increased, you are borderline for redesignation to a higher level institution."

"You cannot afford another write up, Mr. Lacy. As for the other write ups, the committee is going to restrict your canteen privileges for thirty days and early lock up after the four p.m. count for thirty days. Do you have anything you wish to address?"

"No," I answered sullenly.

I would not come to my own understanding until many years later that I was unconsciously channeling negative energy that I harbored for my father, towards authority figures.

Although the various infractions were of a non threatening nature, I had established myself among the staff as a problem inmate.

Once a prisoner is labeled a problem prisoner, the staff has less tolerance for that particular prisoner even to the point of provoking him into reacting so that they, staff, could throw him into the hole, a measure designed to break him from his problematic behavior and keep other prisoners in check at the same time.

Too immature to take advantage of a fair warning, I found myself trapped in a situation where non productive thinking overrode common sense. During one of the early evening lock-in restrictions, I lay in my cell bored, with no knowledge or means to effect positive energy. In search of attention, something inside of me drove me to rebel.

Bam! Bam! Bam! Bam! I kicked on my door for several minutes.

"Ms. Adams, I need to see you up here. I'm in room 327." I shouted out of a small square slot in my door where a window once was.

Ms. Adams was the D-Unit guard on second watch. She was about thirty years old, give or take a few years, white, and at times held a very negative disposition towards convicts. Irritated by the loud kicking I was doing, she marched up to my room giving me the attention I was looking for.

"What do you need Lacy? And stop kicking on my door!" Ms. Adams said, intentionally displaying her nasty attitude that labeled her the bitch she was in the convict's eyes.

"I need for you to let me out my room so I can take a shower," I said wearing a shit-eating grin amused that I had successfully pissed her off.

"Under no terms will you be leaving your room tonight. You are on room restriction," Ms. Adams said walking off obviously annoyed by my frivolous request.

"Forget you then, stupid bitch!" I yelled to deaf ears.

"I know you hear me, trailer trash. Open my door," I screamed over the light chuckles of convicts who had tuned in.

Ms Adams was well aware of my antics; she knew that I was a maladjusted individual who had zero respect for authority, knowing this she intentionally chose to ignore me, which infuriated me even more.

Like a child throwing a tantrum, I began kicking the door again, Bam! Bam! Bam! When I got tired I got on the floor, on my back, so I could kick longer. I kicked for the next ten minutes, nonstop.

Just as I got good and tired, Ms. Adams called the sergeant informing him of my disruptive behavior. She requested I be placed in segregation for disrespect towards a staff member.

I appeared before the committee again.

"Mr. Lacy, you have been before this committee so many times it's ridiculous," the hearing officer stated.

"The staff are singling me out I haven't done anything," I said, unaware of how foolish I sounded.

"Well, your total security points were raised from medium to maximum. We have no choice but to transfer you to a maximum security prison."

"There are only two maximum security prisons in the State of California. You have a choice between San Quentin and Folsom," the hearing officer stated.

The statement startled my twenty year old mind. I had only been familiar with the two prisons through television. I knew the both of them were houses of horrors, equally. They were also playgrounds for some of California's most notorious murderers.

Unlike "Gladiator" school at Tracy, the convicts at San Quentin and Folsom were deadly and wise. It was where murders were common practice for settling disputes; where the Black Guerilla Family was in a nasty war with the Mexican Mafia and Aryan Brotherhood.

My imagery of these two prisons was not good. I thought about my prison conduct over the past few weeks wondering why I could not help myself. Well, it was too late. I had other things to think about; like staying alive. My mind was racing with thoughts of danger and death. I just could not choose between two equally dangerous prisons. The hearing officer's words broke through my trance like thoughts.

"Since you are not able to choose, Lacy, I'll make that choice for you," he said. "I'm putting you in for San Quentin," he continued.

There are a lot of younger inmates there than in Folsom. Besides, it's not all that bad," he added, folding his hands on top each other as if he closed the deal on a luxury cruise.

As I sat before him, I understood what I was facing without having experienced it. There is an instinctual nature in all humans that are confronted with danger or the unknown. It's called "fight or flight" response. I knew I was about to go into a war zone, but I also knew I could not fold.

Chapter 9 San Quentin Prison 1980

San Francisco sits in the Northern part of California; it is a busy city full of diverse cultures and races. One of the city's most visited tourist sites are Fisherman's Wharf, and Alcatraz Island, the infamous federal prison where public enemy number one, Al Capone, had once been confined.

On some main streets you will find refurbished trolley cars shuttling people back and forth around the city. Another piece of San Francisco history is the famous Golden Gate Bridge; it reportedly is the second largest expansion bridge in the United States. The Golden Gate Bridge stretches over the San Francisco Bay. On the south end of the bridge sits a small town named Tamal, California. In this town is one of the most known prisons to man, San Quentin State Prison.

San Quentin sits off the San Francisco Bay with three sides of the prison surrounded by water. It has been functioning as a prison since the 1800's. More than five hundred prisoners there await their fate on death row.

It was a cold, gloomy December in 1980 when I arrived at San Quentin State Prison, via the Grey Goose. The murder count that year had already been thirteen. I was twenty years old. It did not take long for me to know the unwritten codes of convict rules at San Quentin.

Number one was that, convicts at San Quentin played for keeps.

At San Quentin there was no horseplay like at Tracy. No jaw jacking at guards who wore permanent facial expressions of contempt. Childish knife choreographies were nonexistent, human lives were dispensable. If you bump into someone, say excuse me. Never borrow anything from another convict, you may find what you owe triple in value. Most unpaid debts were settled by a shank in your back. Never stare in another convicts cell when you walk past.

I witnessed several acts of violence while at San Quentin. During my first month there, while eating in the dining room, a gun walk guard popped off two rounds from a shotgun into the dining area. After the first shot everyone instinctively dove under the metal kitchen tables for cover. The first shot from any gun walk is a warning, the next is to maim or kill, depending on the circumstance.

It turned out there was a drive by stabbing, a white convict was still sitting, with a metal fork embedded in his neck; his attacker was nowhere to be found. It was my first witness to prison violence.

Another incident happened while housed on the fifth tier, A-Section. My next door neighbor, a Chicano prisoner, had apparently been drinking homemade wine during the four o'clock count. After the count was cleared, the unit officer, tall and lanky, who looked like Gomer Pyle was unlocking cell doors. As soon as he opens the Chicano's cell, the prisoner, obviously in a drunken stupor, lunges at the guard trying to stab him with a sharpened toothbrush.

Gomer Pyle, pulls out his long steel flashlight fending off the attack, then commences to beat the prisoner senseless, never pushing his panic button until the Chicano is down and out. I'm right there, but at a safe distance, looking on in astonishment.

Feeling out of place in the huge structure that seemed like a castle from medieval times, I rotated around other Crips I knew from the neighborhoods of Los Angeles; Bosco, Taco, Mumpy, Big Rick, Herman Moncreif, Ronnie Bamm to name a few. They were youngsters like myself, that had a lot in common with each other, young Crips from L.A., not particularly liked by Black Guerilla Family, 415 Northern California Blacks or Southern California Mexicans. We pulled together, a tight knit circle of disciplined soldiers, initially going under the banner of Blue Magic, founded by James Miller, later restructured as a more organized cadre group, adopting the name Consolidated Crips Organization (CCO).

Meeting on the lower yard bleachers on a Saturday morning, in San Quentin, in 1981, one hundred Crip members from various sets attended forming that alliance. "We need to pull together as one, set aside street beefs for now," Big Bamm from One Eleven Neighborhood said, sounding like a gang chieftain. If anyone doesn't like the idea of organizing as a group under a blue banner then you can get up and leave now, no animosity towards you. But, if you do, you won't flag your colors here. If you ain't with us, you ain't crippin."

The Crips knew and understood this to be a threat, not from the young man who was doing the speaking, but from the consensus of most of the youth who knew it was important for survival as a whole within the confines of one of the most brutal prisons in the nation.

The majority of gang members in attendance were eighteen to twenty five year olds who were at the peak of their gangbanging careers, walking off would have signified cowardice in the eyes of those watching. Each man introduced himself and acknowledged which hood he was from.

The CCO constitution was read and passed around. As always, when men are self imposed into positions of power, it is usually abused. Thus, the idea for organized camaraderie and disciplined ranks vanished no sooner than the ink the constitution was written in dried.

The administration became aware of the Crips uniting as a prison organization and rounded up all documented Crip members, locking them up in C-Section also known as Max Row. The internal fighting, rambling of solidarity, general chaos and abuse of power began.

Max Row was segregated from the general population. The program was basically twenty three hour lock up. On Max Row during the early stages, members consumed a rigid regimen of calisthenics and studies that instilled self discipline. Every other day for two or three hours we participated in group exercises while counting off cadence. The other day we focused on study.

At some point, the line in the ranks, were pushed too hard. We had some fanatics who were holding positions of power who could not think or reason. Members were being stabbed for not wanting to exercise, new arrivals that had no knowledge as to how or why CCO functioned, were stabbed because they chose to not participate. The commissioners sent homies on missions to hit their own homies over CCO business. On more than one occasion situations on Max Row became deadly.

One morning, San Quentin guards escorted our ranks to the segregation yard for rec. At that time we came out our cells all at once, then lined up to go into the sally port five at a time where guards pat searched us.

Rider Keith was getting pat searched before going into the main yard. The guard who performed the pat search was meticulously probing Rider Keith's pockets and noticed he had contraband in his pocket; a thinly rolled marijuana cigarette.

"What's that in your pocket?" the guard asks Keith.

"Nothing," Keith responded.

"Okay, let's have it, empty your pockets," the guard insists.

Keith tries to eat the weed, but the young inexperienced guard is choking Keith so he will not be able to swallow the contraband. All hell breaks loose and fifteen Crips who were in the immediate area rushed the outnumbered guards.

Crips and San Quentin guards were going blow for blow. Boom! Boom! Boom! Boom! echoed the sounds of gun tower guards up above.

The guards held a continuous line of gunfire separating the section that the melee was already taking place, the sally port, and the rec yard, where several more Crips were trying to get to. From the rear additional guards were converging on the area quickly gaining control of the situation.

I was behind Ronnie Bamm, standing at the entrance gate of the rec yard. Ronnie Bamm dived through the barricade of gunfire getting blasted by shotgun pellets in his legs and back, but miraculously got back on his feet to help.

I contemplated a half hearted attempt to join him, but a fusillade of gunfire that ricocheted off the wall I was standing by that caused large pieces of cement chunks to splatter altered that decision for me.

Pop! Pop! Pop! Pop! The .38 caliber pistols cried. Booya! Booya! Booya! Were the sounds of repeater pump shotguns from the cat walk fifteen feet above; order was quickly restored.

Inside the segregation unit the CCO committee was brooding over the fact that all Crip members had not aided and assisted during the melee. They were calling for disciplinary actions for those who had not helped. Crips who were not involved insisted that the line of live gunfire hindered them from getting past the barrier.

The final decision came down that disciplinary action was to be enacted to ensure all members go all out involving warfare, no matter what the sacrifices. Some of the sanctions included doing burpie exercise, running laps, and giving up your television for two weeks.

Suma, one of the CCO generals, who did not care too much for me from day one, was the first to bring me the news that my television had to be confiscated for two weeks by the committee. I bucked because I felt it was personal to Suma. I also didn't think it was justified.

I laced up my state boots tight, donned a pair of workout gloves, telling Suma he could come in and get my television it he wanted it, "I ain't giving nothing up."

At this point it was only me and one other out of fifteen Crips who bucked. Everyone else complied with whatever sanctions they were given. The committee sent Askari down to my cell to handle me, since we were homeboy's. Askari (Floyd Nelson) and I grew up in the same Overhill section of Los Angeles. His street name was Pretty Boy Floyd and later Motor Mouse.

Shortly after becoming CCO he was promoted to General status and was also one of the six committee members who kept the CCO on course.

"Cuz, you read the constitution and you knew what was expected," Askari said to me, defending the CCO sanctions.

"True, but wasn't too much a guy could do under such circumstances. I know damn well you all weren't expecting me to dive through live gunfire, were you?" I shot the rhetorical question at him.

"If you did, you dudes are damn fools," I added.

"Well, damn fools or not, every man knew what was expected of him in any given situation. They sent me at you cuz because if you keep bucking, they are going to move on you," he said revealing his impatience over the matter.

"So are you backing me or not homie, because I ain't feeling this," I said.

"Cuz, you just don't get it, do you?" he said.

"I am on the CCO committee, I roll however they roll."

"Yeah, cuzz, whatever's fair then, homie," I said, angry that this constitution bullshit had clouded his allegiance between homies, and he did not sympathize with me.

The next rec period I walked the yard with the homie Bosco (Ernest Clark). I explained my point of view about the situation and asked him if I rode this thing out could I get his back. Bosco said that it was wrong for Mouse to roll against me, and that he would roll with me if I chose. I thought about a lot of things that night and one of them was I wanted to surround myself with people who were not so quick to turn their back on me.

People who come into prison seeking acceptance in the wrong forms usually regret it in the end. It is always best for a man to put himself in situations that can produce favorable outcomes best suited for him.

In a sense Askari was right, the CCO constitution read that a Crip in distress will be assisted at all cost. By willingly becoming a member of the CCO I put myself in the predicament I was in. I embraced the situation as a lesson in disguise, telling Askari the next morning,

"Cuz, you're right about that situation. I accept my discipline. But, since I don't agree with CCO politics I'm pulling out. I'm really not concerned with the consequences at this point."

Leaving the CCO was a major violation. I was not pushed out nor did I debrief. I am proud to look back and know that I was one of the first to defect on my own accord. Yet, making that decision could have caused me to get "hit".

Eventually, I was sent back into the general population. Months later, the CCO head, Suma, Askari, Big Bamm and other members were sent back to general population due to a ruling in the courts that freed prisoners from doing extended SHU periods just because of gang affiliations.

Over the next year I walked the San Quentin yard keeping anyone who may have been in opposition to me abandoning CCO at arm's length. I walked past Suma and Askari several times a day without us even acknowledging one another. Nothing ever happened. I rotated around a larger group of Crips who were not under paper work; they also had no time for CCO headaches.

I would not be there to witness it, but there was a power struggle between the CCO nucleus and Crips not under paperwork over the next decade.

The power struggle ended up sending the CCO on its head. The last of the CCO diehards and their generals were virtually green lighted. The diehards were attacked whatever yard they walked. What you reap is what you sow.

◆ ◆ ◆

Turmoil continued at San Quentin during the eighties. The year 1982 and 1983 was riot season at San Quentin, at one time there was a stabbing every Sunday for six consecutive weeks. Everyone's nerves were on edge. You did not know where to look for trouble to come from. A continual fog of fear and death hovered over San Quentin never seeming to dissipate.

There was a major riot in 1982. At that time I was housed in C-section, on Max Row, with the CCO's. We had heard multiple gunshots for several minutes. We knew that something big had happened. The story was that several hundred Mexican and White prisoners, who were armed with various makeshift weapons, led a surprise attack on a couple hundred black prisoners. Although the assault was well planned and orchestrated there were no fatalities of the black convicts who were caught off guard.

The entire prison went on lockdown for the remainder of 1982 into 1983. By 1983 I was back in general population and the prison was still on a modified lockdown.

Administration was gradually lifting the lockdown allowing one half day yard privileges testing the waters.

Prior to the 1982 riot, black cliques at San Quentin operated independently of each other.

Mexican and Aryan prisoners took advantage of that disunity by isolating the smaller black cliques and picking them off. The black mindset at the time was that each looked out for his own. However, during the lockdown of 1982 black cliques—Black Guerilla Family, Vanguards, Crips, Bloods and 415—set aside geographical differences plotting the ultimate retaliatory attack. Black cliques set a certain day and time to strike back at enemy prisoners.

On a Saturday, at ten o'clock in the morning, in 1983 the prison deuces sounded off in several sections of the prison where mini attacks were launched in the gym, the security housing unit, as well as the housing units. Four non black prisoners were fatally stabbed on this particular day. Revenge had been swift. The prison enacted another lockdown but I would not see its end. Seven months into that lock down I was transferred to Central Training Facility (Soledad).

By 1984 I was paroled from the war zone environment in the California State Prison system. I filed for divorce shortly before getting out. Chiquita, my wife, had been seeing someone but instead of being open about it as we mutually agreed if it should happen she hid the relationship from me. I may have never found out about this affair if it weren't for me calling home early one morning.

Each morning at 4:00 a.m. I was on the food service wake up list. My cell unlocked I would wait on the bottom floor until the compound officer came to escort a group of workers to the kitchen. Usually I did not call home early morning hours, but recently having cheating dreams involving my wife I wanted to make a surprise call, not to try to catch her in the wrong, but to wake her up with sweet words and tell her how much I loved her.

At this particular time instead of a *she* answering the phone it was a *he*. Chiquita was dead busted. No excuses for a man to be over there at that time of the morning. The damage had been done. Even though I tried to give Chiquita a way to make amends, she refused to discuss it. Making a bad situation worse she changed her phone number. I wrote letter after letter in an attempt to salvage anything that was left. No response. I was left with no other alternative but to file for divorce, irreconcilable differences. I had my cellmate sign her name on the divorce decree since none of my mail to her explaining the divorce had been answered.

Ironically, as soon as I was released from prison Chiquita came up with my current address and phone number. She contacted me but was livid after I explained to her that we were no longer man and wife. She did not understand how I could do such a thing after she had done so much for me during my years in prison. Sending food packages, money and visiting me. It was obvious she was having selective memory. Some women just don't understand, you can't leave out a man's life when he needs you most, then come back when he doesn't need you at all.

Chapter 10 A Taste of Freedom 1985

After spending nearly five years in state prison I was released with no meaningful job skills, no formal education, and was unbroken. At twenty five years old I was surely headed down a road to self destruction. But, you could not tell me that then. It's only fair to say that I did make an honest attempt to get my life in some sort of order.

Although I didn't have a high school diploma I was allowed to enroll in Riverside City College. RCC offered basic education classes through a Pell Grant for students working towards obtaining high school credits needed for either high school diploma or G.E.D. You could then take college credits as well. A student with a Pell Grant also had to work on campus to pay back part of that tuition. I was employed as a part time maintenance worker.

If anyone wishes to meet decent women, enroll in college, you will meet all kind. I could not keep my eyes from roaming. Forrestine was the first female I met at the college. We had a weight training class together and I made the mistake of working out during one of the sessions with my shirt off.

Of course I was penitentiary swoll. It was fatal attraction for Forrestine after that. She approached me asking if I could help her weight train which I complied.

Although Forrestine was good company and she was a free spirited young woman, any other woman I would begin to bond with Forrestine would spoil it for me telling the woman that I was her man. Forrestine had been laying claim unbeknownst to me.

I tried to break the romantic spell Forrestine had for me by using her. It did not work though, anything she could do for me was not enough. However, Forrestine's antics didn't seem to bother Zebby. I met her shortly after meeting Forrestine. Zebby wanted to be around me every chance she could get. Juggling between Forrestine and Zebby, my hands were full.

Needless to say, I was not progressing in terms of getting an education. I simply was not focused. In a short period of time, I embarked upon a crime spree. I had persuaded my female friend to purchase a .22 rifle for me from the surplus store. She was under the impression that I enjoyed hunting rabbit. I sawed off the barrel and the stock of the rifle for easy concealment. I targeted small establishments, expropriating funds to support a care free lifestyle. I was up to my old tricks again.

I held the misconception that as long as I did not hurt anyone during a robbery, since the money did not belong to them, there was no harm in what I was doing. Many years later, having participated in a victim's impact group during incarceration, I learned that the impact of putting someone through a robbery is emotionally devastating. I apologize to any victim who was unfortunate to experience me under these circumstances.

Within a couple months I stopped reporting to my parole officer, going underground in South Central Los Angeles. During this time I foolishly experimented smoking rock cocaine. I had never done this drug before and being away five years in prison I was oblivious to its ability to bring out the worst in the best of people. A woman who I recently became acquainted with named Shari, Shawn, Steve and I were at Shawn's house when I took my first blast. I immediately felt euphoria and bells silently rang in my ears. There was no stopping after that. I was chasing a high that would never satisfy me, I was out there.

I committed robberies more frequently and haphazardly, without any planning whatsoever. I was feeding a drug habit. The cocaine binges were quickly sapping my bankroll, causing me to resort to more desperate measures. Shari, Patrick, who was also a cocaine fiend, and I decided to pull a small heist to get more money after an all-nighter of drinking and getting high.

The Victory Center Post Office sat nestled in a white community in North Hollywood on Lakenshire Boulevard. Its windows were tinted, giving the post office the appearance of a library, quiet and serene. Inside it was bustling with customer activity. The three of us conspired robbing it without realizing that the psychological effects of the cocaine led us to that particular state of desperation.

"Is there any money in a post office?" Shari asked.

"Of course there is," Patrick, the tall thin friend answered, having formulated his opinion on a whim.

115

"Let's park this baby somewhere," I interrupted wanting to kill small talk.

It was a daring attempt to get cash. Shari and Patrick had never robbed before. My uncontrollable desire for the drug dulled any sense of reasoning. I had rationalized that if we could pull it off there would be one endless cocaine party. I looked over at both my confederates and saw that they were both visibly shaken with fear.

"Shit, they're going to bungle this whole thing. I'm going in alone," I decided.

I felt the cold steel of the .38 handgun tucked in my waistband. I picked it up the night before from an associate in the hood.

"It only works sometimes, the cylinder falls out when you pull the trigger," the gang member said, wiping his prints off before handing it to me.

"It doesn't matter my man. I ain't going on no drive by; just trying to get some money."

"Yeah, well make sure you look out for your homie with some dollars after you come up," he responded, trying to sound intimidating.

"Yeah, yeah sure," I lied. Knowing the powerful drug I was using would not allow me to part with any dollars unless it was for more drugs.

"Leave the car running and don't move it for anything," I said to

Patrick, while camouflaging the revolver inside a large manila envelope.

I walked into the lobby noticing there were four customer service lines. In each line stood ten to fifteen customers waiting to either purchase or cash money orders.

Damn, everybody and they mammy is here today. I thought while surveying the scene. The clock on the wall ticked silently, it was 3:20 p.m. I felt myself getting nervous, my palms started sweating. Feeling uneasy, I psyched myself into a sudden surge of confidence.

It's now or never. I thought.

"Don't nobody move!" I heard my own voice scream out, halting a eerie silence.

"This is a robbery," I yelled as if it wasn't obvious enough.

I had complete control. The only control my life symbolized for the moment. As I barked orders, a white male wearing a tropical print shirt and Foster Grant sunglasses watched closely. I held out a manila envelope to each station clerk as they put money in it.

I slowly backed out the door my eyes scanning the lobby area watching out for would be heroes. My eyes shifted briefly towards a man standing aloof, looking too relaxed. I looked away continuing out the door. As I approached the car I could see Patrick at a distance, through the car window, waving his hands frantically, his face contorted as if he were trying to tell me something.

I wondered what could be on his mind at a time like this. Patrick was always in a panic about one thing or another. I thought to myself, I'm gonna shake this dude as soon as I can. Feeling the weight of the money I tried to guesstimate how much I was holding. Suddenly from out of nowhere, a voice yelled.

"Get down! L.A.P.D., do not fucking move!"

I could not believe my ears so I turned slightly, to my surprise the man with the tropical print shirt and another individual were positioned behind parked cars, aiming their firearms directly at me.

Ironically, during the robbery attempt, the two undercover officers had been inside the post office staking the area out. We were unaware, but there had been a recent rash of robberies that caused L.A.P.D. to plant plain clothes officers on alert. Luck was not on our side that day.

It was a nightmare. I could not help but think about the drug I would not be getting. I wished I could just disappear. I swore to myself as I prostrated to the pavement. As I lie there on the sidewalk handcuffed I knew I would not see the streets again anytime real soon. It was the 28th of May, 1985. I had only been out of prison five short months. I cursed myself, I cursed that stupid drug, I cursed everything.

Chapter 11 If These Walls Could Talk

Within seventy-two hours I was arraigned in federal court by a magistrate. The indictment read armed robbery of a post office. I was facing a mandatory twenty-five year sentence based on a grandfather law Congress had enacted in the 1800's called the Jesse James Act. Anyone found guilty of robbing a post office with a gun received a mandatory twenty- five years. I pled out to the federal offense which I hadn't the slightest chance of beating at trial.

Prior to 1987, the length of a federal sentence served was decided by the United States Parole Commission. A prisoner was eligible for parole after serving one-third of any sentence. Prisoners could apply to appear before the parole board every two years until he was deemed fit for parole, or two-thirds of his sentence, in the event parole was never granted.

Several federal prisons span across the nation. When a prisoner is committed to the Bureau of Prisons, the prisoner is subjected to being housed in any one of the many federal prisons. Thus, a prisoner who is from New York could end up serving time in California where he has no friends or family ties.

The Bureau of Prisons has five custody rating levels; minimum (camp), low, medium, high and supermax. The Bureau of Prisons has only one designated Supermax, (Florence ADX), in Florence, Colorado. Opened in 1994 it took the place of the nation's first supermax, United States Penitentiary, Marion, Illinois.

Prisoners are designated according to certain factors; sentence length, age, severity of offense, escape risk, and history of violence. I was designated a high and sent to United States Penitentiary Lompoc in California. I was just sentenced to as much time as I have been living. During my stay at Lompoc prison my conscious mind evoked memories of a torn and battered past while my subconscious mind recorded images of those first years confined behind the walls of federal prison. I remember the senseless violence, the frustrations of prison life causing me to spin out of control.

◆ ◆ ◆

It was June 1987. I had been at Lompoc for a little over a year. My homie, Barry Nelson, had a slight altercation with a member of a rival clique (Bloods), and was wounded with a makeshift weapon. The Bloods member got away but Barry was taken to medical then to the segregation unit. Ironman was the first to get news of the incident. He encountered Milky and me in the prison kitchen.

"Cuzz, Barry was cut by one of the Bloods," Ironman had approached us, emotionally charged.

Ironman, a mutual friend of Barry, Milky and I stood six foot four and weighed two hundred forty pounds of solid muscle. He acquired the name Ironman from the many hours spent on the weight pile pounding out reps, he could do sets with four hundred pounds on the bench press, never seeming to fatigue.

Ironman was doing a life sentence for bank robbery and murder. Although intimidating in size, Ironman was respectful towards his fellow convicts, he generally got along with everyone. You could catch him on the yard jonesing the other convicts.

"Hey Smiley, your nose is so big and wide, a tractor trailer could drive through it," he'd joke. All the convicts within earshot would breakout in laughter.

In a prison setting, you can always count on convicts jonesing on each other, breaking up the monotony of the day. However, there were times when laughter wasn't the best medicine, especially when your loyalty to one of your homies was on the line.

Ironman's words sparked us as if we had been hit with jumper cables. Since the Blood had moved on Barry, someone was expected to retaliate.

"Where is the fool?" Milky responded.

"He's in M-unit," Ironman responded.

"Well, let's go check him in." I added, showing loyalty for my friend and homie.

We sent word for the Bloods shot caller, G-Wine, to meet us on the yard with ol' boy so that we could straighten the matter. Since it was our intent to get ol' boy off the yard one way or another, we carried shanks into the battlefield for precaution.

As we headed towards the east gate that led to the recreation yard we ran into Joe Baby, Newhouse, Lil Calvin and Moon.

They were already aware of the battle that had been brewing, so they accompanied us to the yard, also strapped.

Our rivals were already on the yard waiting for us. As we approached we formed a tight circle around them. Ironman spoke first, "G-Wine," he said, speaking to the clique leader, "Let me holla at you!"

"Go ahead and holla," G-Wine barked back.

"Your boy has to check in, if he leaves the yard, then it won't be no drama," Ironman said sarcastically, like a true prison spokesman.

In a prison environment where aggression runs rampant and the norm has zero understanding, one must not show any sign of weakness. G-Wine, wanting to see where his homies heart was, responded with hostility. "Well, that's on him. He ain't gotta go nowhere if he don't want to."

The dialogue was cold as were the daggers in the eyes of the combatants. The young Blood that had been the center of all the drama moved first. Stepping forward he pulled his hands out from under his jacket revealing a pipe in one hand, and a crudely made shank in the other.

"I ain't going nowhere!" he yelled, swinging the weapons inside the tight circle of convicts.

Ironman, Milky and I pulled out makeshift shanks. Ironman rushed towards the Blood, weapon in hand. I followed suit. The other gang members fled in fear; every one of them except for G-Wine, who stood his ground like a soldier. He had no weapon, but defiance in his eyes.

Ironman backed off quickly. G-Wine stood posted, our eyes locked. G-Wine knew he was vulnerable to an attack not being strapped. I respected G-Wine's bravery for not showing fear. I ran past him towards my intended target. We swung and lunged at each other like Roman Gladiators.

I was determined to get at him, my adrenaline was flowing. During one of his down swings I noticed he left his upper left side unprotected. I lunged with the shank penetrating it in his neck, causing blood to gush out the open wound like a running faucet.

"Aw, blood, you stuck me!" he shouted in disbelief, as if for some insane reason we had been playing a game.

Guards, who had been peering through binoculars from the guard towers, sounded off the deuces. The running sound of feet and the jingling of keys alerted me that guards would soon pour onto the scene securing the area then detaining anyone who even looked guilty.

Feeling vindicated for what I had come to settle, I dropped my weapon and turned to walk away.

By then the guards had already converged on the scene.

All of the other combatants had slipped away long before the deuces were sounded, so it was just me and the Blood.

"Secure the area, get down!" the goon squad commanded rushing towards me putting me in handcuffs taking me to segregation.

The Blood was escorted to the hospital. As I lay in my bunk in segregation I tried to sort out how it all happened.

It all came down to a matter of hood respect basically. We were all for one and one for all. I felt like a warrior having gone into battle coming out victorious, my adrenaline was still flowing, exhaustion set in and I fell asleep.

◆ ◆ ◆

"Lacy, Lacy," a voice called out as I turned over in my sleep.

I thought I was dreaming until opening my eyes hearing it clearer.

"Yeah, What up?" I answered back.

"It's Ironman, homie," he said sounding a little distant.

"Ironman?" I asked, puzzled.

"What are you doing over here homie? I thought you had gotten away?" I asked.

"Some rat snitched me out saying I was involved with that incident."

"What cell you in, Iron?"

"I'm in cell #8, listen I need to tell you something," he said; the tone of his voice indicating something serious.

"Go ahead," I listened closely.

"Ol' boy died at the hospital," Ironman blurted out not caring who had been listening to us.

My heart jumped and I grew quiet. I quickly surmised the possibility of me never seeing the streets again. At that moment I did not feel like a warrior. I felt foolish and scared. Damn, I thought.

"For reals?" I asked, noticing a slight cracking sound in my voice. I only spoke to fill the void quickly regretting it.

"Psych!" Ironman screamed as he broke up in laughter.

"I was just kidding, homie. Scared your ass, huh?" he added.

I forgot this fool is a practical joker. I thought. "Scared my ass, fool. I ain't tripping on that."

He really had jolted me. I had exposed fear and hoped that no one else noticed.

"I'm going back to sleep," I added.

Damn, what if ol' boy would have died? I pondered different scenarios about it and how it would have turned out as I drifted off to sleep.

In segregation, days seem endless; you can't really tell one day from the next. Convicts stay up all night shouting at each other from cells about anything and everything. You can gauge the time of day whether it is morning, afternoon or evening from the meals that are served. Others sell wolf tickets. Selling wolf tickets is shouting threats at other convicts from within the safety of your cell without any intention whatsoever of carrying out those threats.

Convicts who have no associates they can jive with scream animal sounds. For example; barking like a dog, bird whistling or other weird noises to keep the insanity of isolation from getting to their heads.

"Lacy!" the guard said awaking me as he peered in my darkened cell.

"Yeah, what?" I answered.

"You're getting a cellmate," he said.

"I don't want a cellmate," I responded, annoyed.

"Well, you don't have a choice. He's assigned to this cell and this is where I'm putting him," the guard sneered.

Well, if you put him in here with me, you'll be reassigning him to the outside hospital," I said angrily.

"I'm writing you up and reporting it to the Lieutenant that you are refusing a cellmate," the agitated guard warned.

"Yeah, yeah, whatever," I responded showing unconcern.

The guard stormed off with the convict in tow to his superior's office down the range.

"Lt. Keller," the guard whined. "An inmate down the tier is refusing a cellmate."

"Who is the inmate?" asked the Lieutenant.

"Inmate Lacy," the guard answered.

"Well, reassign the inmate to another cell. Lacy is under investigation for the stabbing of another inmate. He is to get no cellmates at this time," the Lieutenant ordered.

"Yes sir," the guard responded meekly.

Looking through a hand mirror I held out the cell bars, I could see the guard escorting the inmate back down the tier. As he walked by my cell, he shot daggers at me as if he took it personally. I agitated the situation more by saying,

"Hey asshole," aloud so that the other convicts could hear me.

"Where's my cellie?"

Later that night while lying on my bunk, I pulled a porno mag from under the worn mattress. After flipping through the pages, I lubricated my manhood with petroleum jelly and masturbated. I fantasized about women I had prior sexual relationships with and other women I found sexually appealing. Closing my eyes I drifted off into a deep sleep.

◆ ◆ ◆

During the following month I received packages from the homies in the population via the orderlies who worked the segregation unit.

"Lacy!" the orderly yelled as he slid the folded kite under my door. A kite is a triangular shaped folded paper with a message written in it.

Unfolding the kite I read its message,

> What's up homie? Much respect to you for going down for me. If you need anything I'm on C range.
> Your homie, Barry.

Another read:

> "We are sending you a radio, batteries, stamps and snacks through the orderly. Be looking out for it. Stay up!
> The homies, Moon and Milky.

When a convict catches a stabbing, he becomes penitentiary gossip for several years. His status among the yard becomes one of respect and fear.

"Did you hear about Lacy stabbing ol boy?" a convict said to his roadie on the yard.

"Yeah man, that nigga ain't to be messed with."

Because of the overnight celebrity status I earned, I used it to my advantage exploiting those who knew that I was capable of inflicting violence.

"Hey Money," Moon said to the light skinned player from the San Fernando Valley.

"Yeah, playa," he answered.

"I got a kite from Lace. He told me to get at you and see if you could send him a carton of Camels."

"Lacy doesn't even smoke my man," Money replied seeing it was a long range extortion attempt.

The message got back to me via the orderly. Allowing all of the attention to get to my head I sent a scathing response.

"Money, you are a punk. Whenever I get back to population it's on."

Within the next couple of weeks two guards came to my cell to escort me to the disciplinary hearing officer.

"Lacy, get dressed. You're going to DHO," one of the guards told me as they stood waiting impatiently for me to get ready.

"A--ight, that means I should be getting out today," I said aloud, but to no one in particular.

At the hearing there were three staff members including my staff representative who was there to report that I had been programming and not been in any serious trouble until now.

"Mr. Lacy, would you like to tell us what happened?"

"Yeah, I've been in here for almost ninety days and have not seen anyone until now. I don't even know what I'm in here for," I lied with a straight face.

The hearing officer's eyebrows raised suspiciously.

"Are you saying you have not received a copy of your write up?"

"No, Sir," I answered.

The statement I gave him was partly true. I had not received any incident report yet because I had been under investigation, but I knew damn well what they had me for.

"Okay, I'm going to read your charges to you," he says.

"On June 17, 1987 I saw several inmates on the rec yard grouping up. Suddenly the group dispersed and I saw two inmates fighting with weapons. One of those inmates was later identified as inmate Lacy, James #81770-012."

"That's a lie," I said clearly agitated about being witnessed by a staff member.

"Who wrote that?" I asked.

"Officer Jeffries in gun tower #3," the hearing officer responded.

"How do you plead, Mr. Lacy?"

"Not guilty," I plead as I sunk down in the chair, shoulders slumped.

"Due to eyewitness statements and information from confidential informants, I'm finding you guilty. I'm sentencing you to sixty days disciplinary segregation. I also recommend a disciplinary transfer to a more secure facility."

"Are you a member of the Crips," he asked.

"No, Sir," I answered.

"Okay, Mr. Lacy, that concludes this hearing."

Assholes. I thought.

After getting escorted back to my cell, I thought about the hearing that had just taken place.

I wondered why it was so important that the administration wanted me transferred, especially when everyone knew the victim would not be going back to population. I also learned that in order for the administration to classify me as a gang member it either had to be documented in my prison file or I had to admit membership.

131

Once the administration validated you a gang member you were subject to be locked up any time there was a beef on the yard between enemy cliques. Other unnecessary harassment came with this tag as well. From earlier experiences I learned it was not wise to confirm what any authority questioned you about, particularly if that information could incriminate you. For example, what could I gain by letting them on that I was affiliated with a gang? If they already had this information they would not be asking me.

Some concerned individuals on the tier with me called out, "Hey Lace, what happened at your hearing today?"

"They're going to let me back out in population after I do my seg time," I lied.

Within the next few days a kite was slid under my door,

"Lacy, this is Money. I sent you a carton of smokes through the orderly. You should get them sometime tonight."

As I read the kite I smiled. Damn, word sure travels fast around here. If you want everyone in prison to know your business tell another inmate, he'll tell another and so on. Inmates gossip regularly. Often times when there is no new information to gossip about the fabricate gossip.

These are bitter hearted inmates who find it hard to mind their own business. Misery loves company. I knew that once my message was indirectly relayed about me supposedly getting out of segregation, the news would be all over the compound. It would of course find the ears of Money too. It was a well crafted ploy that worked to my advantage.

The following weeks, inmates whom I sent previous kites asking for assistance suddenly sent cigarettes, stamps and coffee. A pack of smokes were equal in value to their price sold at the prison commissary. For example, if a pack cost three dollars then you could barter the cigarettes for three dollars in goods. You could buy anything of value; snacks, toiletries, drugs, shanks or prison brew. The medium of exchange now is postage stamps.

Very few comforts can erase the tension or uncomfortable feeling of being isolated. While awaiting transfer I grew increasingly frustrated. I started having fleeting thoughts about what a mistake I had made. It was not a wise choice to assault the convict on the open yard in front of so many witnesses. Now that it was all said and done, I was a little perturbed that the other homies were not as overzealous in defending our neighborhood camaraderie. Even Ironman had been released back to population after the investigation. No staff member could place him at the scene of the attack.

The unit manager made his weekly rounds in seg.

"Mr. York! I need to see you down here," I yelled out from within the confines of my cage.

"Oh, Mr. Lacy," he said.

"I came over to inform you that your transfer order came back today, you are designated to Leavenworth Penitentiary."

"In Kansas! Leavenworth, Kansas. I'm from California, Mr. York. There's no way my family will be able to travel that distance to visit."

"That's not our problem, Mr. Lacy. You have demonstrated that you require greater security needs than we have here. It's a decision coming down from Region."

"That's messed up, Mr. York, I ain't done anything," I whined.

"Now what did you want to see me about Mr. Lacy."

"Never mind," I mumbled.

I sat up most the night wondering what the maximum security facility would be like. Unlike Lompoc Federal Prison where the compound housed mainly convicts from the Westcoast, United States Penitentiary Leavenworth comprised mostly Eastcoast convicts.

In particular there was a standing beef between Washington D.C. and California blacks. The feud dated back years ago, there were several incidents of murder on both sides. At Lompoc, during the time I was there, I had only seen isolated incidents of violence. Nothing out of the ordinary for a maximum security prison. However, there a large influx of D.C. prisoners arriving at Lompoc penitentiary, heightening the climate for drama. Some believed the administration was intentionally manipulating the numbers. Cliques warring with each other on prison compounds always allowed the administration to maintain control.

I would not be there at the time, having been transferred, but several years later, the riot that had been slowly fermenting had finally reached its ugly head. Vamp, a Hoover Crip, got into an altercation with one of the D.C. boys. The D.C. pulled out a shank an attempted to stab Vamp. Vamp, slightly wounded, retreated to his unit. Clarence Hoover, an undisputed shot caller for the Crips, set the tone for retaliation.

"These D.C. boys are way out of line," Big Hoover said.

The D.C. boys who were also on edge, heard rumor of a plot building to move on their group. Somehow both cliques agreed to settle it on the rec yard. Foolishly believing they were going to a battle without weapons, Crip and Blood members mobbed to the prison yard and found themselves in an ambush. They were met by rivals wielding weight bars and makeshift weaponry.

The two enemy factions locked in a bloody embrace. No one was seriously hurt. I'd become aware of this riotous affair through prison grapevine while I was housed in U.S.P. Lewisburg in Pennsylvania, a stronghold for the D.C. clique.

Chapter 12 Leavenworth Federal Prison

A bus load of Lompoc convicts who were being transferred out of Lompoc penitentiary for one reason or another, were driven to Vandenberg Air Force Base air strip. Of course I was one of the unfortunate passengers. We awaited a plane that would transport everyone to a transfer hub center in El Reno, Oklahoma. At El Reno, convicts were transported like slaves on the shores of South Carolina in the 1700s.

Depending on your destination it could take weeks to get there. During transportation convicts wore waist chains, handcuffs and leg shackles. Eating periods consisted of a dry cheese sandwich, apple and a small juice. There was no comfort while eating and traveling wearing these restraints. After one week you grow mentally fatigued, your body wears down. Someone coined the term "Diesel Therapy" to describe the inhumane effects on the convicts.

It was 1987 when I arrived at Leavenworth, one of the nation's oldest federal prisons. Its frontal view has the appearance of the Capitol building in Washington D.C. It had a huge dome on top the roof, several giant concrete steps leading to the front entrance. Leavenworth looked like a fortress, 45ft high walls, manned gun towers with guards carrying automatic assault weapons and high power rifles. In the 1800s,

Leavenworth was a military prison.

It later became a prison for convicted felons as federal offenses were rapidly being committed. Leavenworth has its history. It held many famous and not so famous convicts during its existence. Marcus Garvey, a black Jamaican, who was a black nationalist, formed the United Negro Improvement Association in New York, 1917. He preached to American blacks that they would only be respected if they were economically strong. Garvey's emphasis was to take as many blacks back to Africa who wanted to go. Another notable figure in Leavenworth's history was Elijah Muhammad. The Nation of Islam leader also preached for blacks to uplift themselves and to become independent of the white man, he was sent to Leavenworth Federal Prison after refusing to sign up for the armed forces draft.

Movie goers would be familiar with "Birdman" of Alcatraz. Robert Stroud, had first taken interest in the anatomy of birds while in Leavenworth prison. Birdman poured over medical books on birds and became well known in the veterinary society. He wrote several essays on the topic, his writings were respected in the field of veterinary medicine. Birdman murdered a guard while at Leavenworth and then was sent to Alcatraz Island.

In the mid eighties, legislators focused on America's drug problems that affected society as a whole. As a result Congress enacted Draconian laws that filled the nation's prisons with street drug traffickers. The war on drugs had targeted the minorities who had no resources for getting significant quantities of drugs to America. Of the new wave traffickers were Bo Bennet, Freeway Rick, Ray Ray Browning from Los Angeles and Pasadena California, Raful Edmunds from D.C., Felix Mitchell from Oakland, California and many others. Felix controlled a major housing project distributing heroin and cocaine, becoming a millionaire many times over. Mitchell was indicted under the R.I.C.O. act, convicted to a life sentence and sent to Leavenworth Federal Prison.

While in Leavenworth, Felix Mitchell had a dispute over money with another convict. Later, Felix Mitchell, was stabbed as he slept. Mitchell, still alive, was sent to the outside hospital where he later died from his wounds. In an ironic set of circumstances, an appeal of his life   sentence had been granted just days before his untimely death. It all seemed strange as I was briefed on Leavenworth politics. Felix had been murdered one year before I arrived.

A group of us, new cons, were escorted through the huge rotunda area out into the main corridor.

"Anderson, Bailey, Jackson, and Lacy, grab a bedroll you are assigned to B cell house," the guard yelled.

Carrying our bedrolls, we filed into the huge cell house. The tiers were five stories high on both sides. On each tier were long rows of rooms that were double bunked, a few of them single. The rooms had thick doors that were a barrier from constant noise. Yet, at times one could still hear shouting, domino games and continuous chatter.

"Domino! Nigga," an inmate screamed as if he were in a recreation center.

I could not understand how easily the word nigga could be uttered from any African American's vocabulary. Civil rights activist of the turbulent sixties fought hard to erase that demeaning stigma that caused blacks to feel inferior.

George Jackson would have turned over in his grave having heard the word used by blacks so loosely. Comrade George Jackson, prison activist and revolutionary during the sixties and seventies stood up against racism inside the walls of the California prison system.

George spent eleven years in prison, seven of them in solitary confinement. He read voraciously on authors; Mao Tse Tung, Karl Marx, Che Guvera, Patrice Lumbumba, Franz Fanon and other revolutionary literature. He became inspired by their theory and ideology transforming his own character from one of reactionary to revolutionary.

George Jackson called for unity among black, brown and white inmates alike.

"The keepers are our enemies," George would say. George never faltered on his principles.

"Lacy, take your bedroll, your assigned to the fifth tier you are going to cell #529," the guard at the office said.

As I walked up the winding staircase in B-upper I was a little nervous about being in a different state where I knew no one. I reached the fifth tier.

"Let me see 518, 523, okay here it is 529," I said aloud.

The occupant of the room was not there so I went in looking around the cell. I could tell that a brother lived there. On his picture board were Jet "Beauty of the Week" centerfolds. On another board were family photos. Must be his wife and kids I thought.

I placed my bedroll on the top bunk. I had intended to wait for the bunkie to show before I unrolled my bedroll. Typically prisoners as a show of respect waited to be welcomed by the occupant of the room before just moving right in. You want to give the prisoner who has been living there the opportunity to accept you.

At around the same time I put my bedroll down the door opened. I turned around to see a convict looking me up and down with a sign of disapproval as if he were agitated about something. As he walked out shutting the door back I could hear him yell down the tier, "Yo, Jersey, you got a cellmate."

A tall, slim convict, who had on a baseball cap cocked sideways, pranced through the door.

"Yo, man," he said.

"I got my main man moving in here, so don't get too comfortable. We're putting for a room change today," the slim convict said.

"Yeah, okay; no problem. Just let me know when," I responded agreeably.

I was beginning to feel my arrival on a sour note. The convict from Jersey was clearly agitated that I had been moved into his room, which of course I had no control of. We had not even formally introduced ourselves to one another and there was already resentment harboring.

That day we spoke few words. In the prison setting, blacks did not openly embrace new arrivals like other ethnic groups who would have open arms for their own. Brothers only extended this gesture with someone from their neighborhood or a close friend. If a black knew no one upon arriving in a prison, he would generally have to fend for self. I was slowly becoming aware that this had been a backlash of slavery where slaves were brainwashed into hating their own. A slave that was divided was easily controlled by the master.

I decided to give Slim some space. The next morning at breakfast line I asked another convict in line, "Where do the guys from Cali eat?"

"Over there youngster; near the front," the older con answered.

"Thanks man," I replied genuinely.

"You from Cali?" he asked me.

"Yeah," I answered.

"I know your homie Big Hoover. Walk over with me, I'll show you who he is so you can meet the rest of your homies," he offered.

"Good looking out," I said.

We walked over to an area where the California homies sat, "Hey Hoover, this is your homie. He just got here."

"I'm Lacy," I said extending my hand for a greeting.

"Big Hoov," he said shaking my hand.

"These are the homies, we all from Cali."

"What's up homies?"

"Hey, what up?" they sung back.

"Where you coming from?" Big Hoov asked.

"Lompoc," I answered.

"Yeah, I put in for a transfer to go there," Big Hoov stated excitedly.

"Did you know Joe Baby and Calvin?" a homie named Little John asked.

"Yeah, man, real cool people. They still there," I answered.

"You need anything?" Lynn Brazille interjected.

"Of course he do, fool," Hoover replied for me.

"He'll hook you up a care package, homie. Meet us on the yard next move," another homie named Simone offered. "Aight homie," I agreed.

Later that day I ran into Halisi, a convict I knew from Lompoc prison. Halisi was a red brother; he sported a huge brownish-reddish afro hairstyle. He was quiet and well disciplined. Halisi was from San Diego, California and a devoted member of the Black Guerilla Family. Halisi was also anti-social towards most convicts, he kept to himself. We befriended one another in Lompoc penitentiary through discussing black literature, George Jackson's books in particular; Soledad Brother and Blood in my Eye.

"What's up comrade?" Halisi greeted me.

"Good to see you again, my friend," I answered.

"What they ship you here for?" Halisi asked concerned.

"I stabbed a guy," I bragged.

"Yeah, well, watch yourself around here brother, these guys ain't no good," he said.

I didn't question the statement because I knew Halisi had an embedded mistrust for anyone he wasn't familiar with. Thus, his response was not unusual.

"Have you met Razor yet?" Halisi asked.

"Naw, I haven't met all of the homies."

144

Halisi and I encountered Razor on the recreation yard.

"Razor," Halisi called out upon seeing him doing chin ups .

"Greetings comrade," Razor answered.

"We have a new homie here, he's from L.A."

"What's up, brother," I said to him.

"I'm Razor," he said with a firm handshake.

"Righteous," I said.

"I'm Lacy."

Razor was a ranking member of the Black Guerilla Family. He was well respected in the Bay area. He had arrived to Leavenworth from the California prison system, via Pelican Bay supermax. Razor reminded me of a Zulu Warrior. Razor was also an avid reader of revolutionary material, he was politically astute and we would discuss the current situation in regard to black people.

"Comrade, if you want to come out on weekends with Halisi and I, we run laps and do calisthenics," Razor offered.

"What type of calisthenics do you all do?" I asked.

"Different variations of burpies—five, seven and ten counts. We also do jumping jacks, sit-ups, push-ups etc."

"Yeah, sure, okay. I will bust down with you all," I answered.

"Join us Saturday morning on the yard?"

"I'll be there," I answered with certainty. Feeling that I had just been challenged and not wanting to duck rec.

◆ ◆ ◆

Back at the cellhouse, the situation between me and my roommate was getting intolerable.

Bam! Bam! Bam! "Come on cellie, damn, I need to get something," Slim lashed out.

I was sitting on the toilet with an oblong piece of cardboard blocking the window of the door for privacy while I was handling my business.

Damn. My heart jumped as I was startled by the knocking. This fool is really pushing it. I thought. After using the bathroom, and by now agitated, I yelled to Slim who had taken off halfway down the tier.

"Hey Slim!"

"Yo, what's up?" Slim answered sarcastically.

"Check it out Slim," I said unable to mask the anger in my voice.

A few convicts who had been hanging around had their antenna like ears tuned in.

Slim stepped into the room.

"What's up man, is that you are disrespecting me while I was trying to handle my business," I said while stepping towards Slim.

"You out of line Slim. Ain't nothing that important that you can't wait on a man to take a dump. Man don't ever do that bullshit again," I added.

Though I had not really crossed the line with Slim during the confrontation, Slim had been lightweight checked. I gave the convict respect and space every since moving in the cell. However, Slim annoyed the counselor so much that the counselor intentionally delayed moving his homie into the cell with him. It left Slim angry and he was acting ignorant with me for no reason.

Later that night, Slim kept himself up most the night almost to 2:00 a.m. supposedly reading. Though he had his eyes closed.

I know this asshole is keeping me up out of spite, I thought.

"Hey, Slim, you finished with the light?" I said while trying to repress the contempt in my voice.

"Naw man, I'm reading," Slim answered in a snide manner.

I got up out the bed flicking the light switch off. "Hey, man, what's up?"

"I told you I wasn't through with the light yet," Slim said apparently annoyed.

"I heard you the first time, my man, and if you cut that light back on we gonna touch everything in this room," I said facing Slim in the dimly lit room.

Slim failed to meet the challenge. He realized from the earlier encounter we had that I was not selling wolf tickets. Something in my eyes gave warning he should retreat. Slim, folded his book closed and lay quietly in the darkness.

I held the shank with a firm grip under the blanket, never exposing it. You never should underestimate any man, and never challenge a man without the expectation of that challenge being faded. Damn, I allowed this fool to get me off square. It would not be until morning that I fell asleep, unable to fight it off any longer. Slim's antics came to a screeching halt.

A few days later Big Hoover approached me.

"Hey homie, I'm transferring tomorrow morning. I'm going to Lompoc," Big Hoover smiled.

"Give my greetings to the homies, Big Hoov."

"Hey, look," Hoov said.

"Since I'm leaving, see if the counselor will move you in with my little brother."

Big Hoov's brother was not from Cali. He was from Oklahoma. They were co-defendants on a bank robbery. They were like night and day in terms of character. Lil Hoov was nothing like his brother. I contemplated moving in with him for a minute. I thought about staying on to torment my cellie, but quickly decided it would just be a waste of energy.

"Sounds like a good idea to me, Hoov," I finally said. "Ask your brother to put in the request for us," I added.

It wasn't twenty four hours later after I moved in with Lil Hoov that I was summoned to the Lieutenant's office.

"James Lacy, report to the front desk," the factory manager called over the P.A. system.

"Yeah, Lacy here," I said standing in front of the foreman's desk.

"You're wanted in the Lieutenant's office," he said unconcerned.

"What for?" I asked sensing some sort of trouble.

"I don't know, but here is your pass."

When an inmate is summoned to the Lieutenant's office it's not a good thing.

Knock, knock. I tapped nervously on the door.

"Come in," a voice answered.

"Sit down," the Lieutenant stated, seemingly bothered by my

presence.

"Who are you?" he asked.

"I'm Lacy. My supervisor said you called for me."

"Yeah, yeah, Lacy, have a seat. I have a write-up for you," he said while thumbing through his papers.

"Write-up?" I responded in a high pitch.

The Lieutenant showed me a picture of a shank laying aside a ruler indicating the shank to be nine inches long.

"Have you ever seen this weapon before?" he asked.

"No, I haven't," I answered displaying a confused look.

"Well, Mr. Lacy, you see these shower shoes?" he went on.

"This shank fits right here perfect. Your unit officer says he found them in you and Hoover's cell," he said, referring to Lil Hoover.

The shower shoes were a pliable beach type thong with extra thick cushiony foam sole. The foam sole had been carefully sliced in half and a groove cut in one half where the shank fit perfectly. It then had been glued back together. The weight of the shower shoe was how it was discovered.

"Well, it could not possibly be mine, cause I just moved into that room yesterday," I said without thinking how absurd that particular

150

remark was.

"Mr. Lacy, I'm having you placed in segregation. Your cellmate is there also. Perhaps the two of you can get your stories together and tell us who the weapon belongs to."

Damn! I cursed under my breath. I had knowledge of Lil Hoover having a weapon. However, the weapon was his. Not mine. Prison protocol dictated that ownership of contraband inside a cell was nine tenths of the law. I assumed that since it was his knife he would ride his beef. No sense two convicts going down for one weapon. However, we were separated while in segregation and never had the opportunity to get our stories straight. He denied knowing anything about the weapon and so did I.

Turned out Lil Hoov had some outstanding debts. With his brother no longer there to protect him, either someone dropped a note on Lil Hoov or he dropped one on himself.

During the procedure of locking Hoov up and securing his property the shower shoe knife was discovered and I went down with him. Damn fool I thought, upon hearing the scenario about my own situation through grapevine news.

At this point I felt frustrated. A weapons infraction after being transferred for a stabbing does not look good.

Yet, it would have been against everything I believed to tell the Lt.

that the weapon was his not mine.

"If I bust his head open about this, I'd be playing right into the administrator's hands."

I spent the next forty five days in disciplinary segregation. Being in segregation set back any positive goals I had intent on accomplishing on the compound at Leavenworth. Administration had viewed my prison file and noticed I had recently been transferred to Leavenworth from Lompoc for a serious assault. Administrators recommended me transferred out of Leavenworth. It was no more than what I expected.

No matter how much I wanted to conform there always seemed to be traps in my path. I arrived to Leavenworth with goals on getting my G.E.D. and was enrolled in the drug program. For the weapon infraction I was re-designated to United States Penitentiary Lewisburg in Pennsylvania. It was the furthest east of all the penitentiaries which housed maximum security convicts. I sent a message by a convict going back to the compound.

"Hey, main man! Let me holla at you one minute," I yelled out my cell to the convict being released from the hole."

"Yeah, What up California?" the convict answered having recognized my voice.

"Do you know who Lil Hoover is?" I asked.

"Yeah, I know him."

"Give him a message for me. Tell him that's messed up he didn't take his beef. He's a cold piece of work."

"Alright soldier, I'll make sure he gets your message," the convict said, hurrying down the tier not wanting to spend any more time than he already had in the hole.

Chapter 13 USP Lewisburg 1988

Lewisburg federal prison was a D.C. stronghold. It was one of the most violent institutions in the federal system. The prison housed eleven hundred maximum security prisoners in an open population. Seventy five percent of the convict population was black. The administration had a hands-off policy concerning the handling of prisoners. Punchy, a D.C. prisoner seemed to have been literally running the compound with the D.C. clique. During his twenty year incarceration, Punchy had earned a reputation as a shot caller within the D.C. ranks. Five cliques made up most of the consensus of the black population; D.C., Maryland, New York, Philly and Boston. There were also Cubans, Dominicans and a tight knit group of Italian mobsters.

The red brick wall that secured the perimeter at Lewisburg prison was less than half the size of Leavenworth's wall. It almost seemed as if one could get a running start he could jump as high as he could, grab the top of the wall, pulling himself over. Mind you, that's what it seemed like.

I'm sure it was one of those distorted image trips. Every prisoner at one time or another fantasizes about escaping. Few dare try. The penalty for an escape or attempt is five years added to one's current sentence. Make it or not. Yet, for reasons unknown, many lifers and long term prisoners choose to serve their sentences as opposed to trying a hand at freedom.

The bus pulled into the sally port. I knew what to expect from my previous arrivals at various prisons. We would be met by a armada of menacing guards who would bark orders for everyone to strip naked, bend over, spread their ass cheeks and cough. No matter how many times I went through this it would always piss me off the same as if it were the very first time. Absolutely degrading. Not one time could I remember hearing about any contraband falling out of a inmate's ass during one of these searches.

This shit sucks, I was thinking as the guards prying eyes molested me while I faked a cough. As normal procedures for disciplinary transfers, I was taken to segregation for a scheduled Captain's review which was normally held within a day or two. The interview was routine. The Captain of the prison would peruse your file asking you questions to determine whether or not you would be a threat on his compound.

"Is there any reason you can't go to general population?" Captain Thomas asked me.

"No," I replied. Unsure whether he would interpret that I could or I couldn't.

"You will be released to the general population today," he responded still thumbing through my file affirming that I had given the right answer.

If a man is a man at heart, he respects others, and stands strong; he will usually get that respect in return. If he doesn't, a man got to do what a man's got to do.

A few hours after appearing before the Captain I was let out into the busy corridor. Unlike Leavenworth, no guard escorted me to the unit I had been assigned. The guard simply told me that I would be going to I-Unit, an orientation unit for new arrivals. I thought it odd for the guard to let me out without telling me where I-Unit was located.

It was during the evening meal so looking down the corridor was like Times Square on New Year's Eve. Hundreds of convicts were milling around. As I walked down the busy corridor with my bedroll I shifted myself back and forth unsure which direction to go. No one was paying any attention to me, these convicts seemed to be hurried and pre-occupied.

I saw one convict hand another a small tin foil package, that convict gave the man four cartons of Camels in return. I assumed from seeing these kinds of transactions in the past heroin was being sold. Damn, I thought. A drug transaction right under the guards nose, in the main corridor. The guard standing nearby had been staring into space as if he were not even there.

"Keep moving," a guard said to a group of young convicts, minus the confidence in his voice.

"Fuck You!" the youngsters chimed back in unison not even budging.

It was very obvious the administrators did not have control of Lewisburg penitentiary. The sea of faces was alien to me as I dodged in and out of traffic. Suddenly, I recognized someone. A youngster sporting a fresh shiner appeared smiling.

"What's up Tim?" I called out.

"Hey, California. What's happening my man," Tim greeted shaking my hand.

Tim Holiday was from D.C. He was not biased towards the California clique because of already having experienced the drama of another geographical war.

In F.C.I. Petersburg, Virginia, Tim Holiday beat down a convict from New York. Tim was good with his hands. He had gotten out on the convict by cutting his face open with a three piece. In a retaliatory move, the New York crew summoned the D.C. boys out to the recreation yard. A common place for settling disputes.

The brawl turned deadly when during the chaos, a staff member had been innocently killed by an overzealous prisoner swinging a crudely made shank. Tim Holiday and two others were indicted for the murder. They were given life sentences.

"Where you coming from Cali?" he asked.

"Leavenworth," I answered, looking weary from the bus ride.

"You need anything?" Tim asked.

"I'll holla at you if I do, Tim. Thanks anyway," I said knowing it would not be until at least a week before I received my personal property.

It was wise not to accept everything that was offered in prison, even if you were familiar with the giver.

"What unit they put you in?" Tim asked, insisting on being resourceful.

"I-Unit," I answered with an expression that needed directions.

"Come on Tim!" his homeboy yelled, impatiently waiting while Tim and I exchanged greetings.

"I-Unit is all the way on the other end of the corridor, the very last unit on the left," Tim shouted as he picked up his step to catch up with his partner.

"Right on Tim. Thanks," I yelled back.

A couple weeks after being in I-unit where there were no homies, a new arrival from California would be housed with me. The legendary Doc Holliday. Doc, (no relation to Tim Holiday) was known among many in the California prison system.

Doc had been incarcerated in the California prison system during the turbulent sixties and seventies. Repressive conditions motivated a tight knit group of black prisoners, organized by W.L. Nolen, George Jackson and others to form what was later called The Black Guerilla Family.

The BGF formed to battle racist attacks by white and Mexican prisoners. The BGF practiced self discipline and adopted revolutionary ideologies. Racist prison guards were always known to have a hand in assisting in the annihilation of black prisoners, so when W.L. Nolen, Cleveland Edwards and Alvin Miller, black prisoners who were gunned down in cold blood on the Soledad exercise yard. The penalty for brawling with white prisoners, a Soledad prison guard was beaten and thrown over the third tier in retaliation.

George Jackson, Fleeta Drumgo and John Clutchette, Black Guerillas, were charged with the guard's murder. This symbolized "Soledad Brothers", three Soledad prisoners facing execution for a prison guard's death. The trio was transferred to San Quentin prison to face trial. Two days before they were to start trial George Jackson was killed during a takeover of the Adjustment Center cell block. Those chain of events catapulted George into martyrdom affecting his remembrance as legendary. Doc Holliday had been one of many prisoners after George's death that was committed to Comrade George's call for black unity and strength.

However, that era started changing and the state was no longer producing W.L. Nolens and George Jackson's. Instead a lot of new jacks were flooding the California prison system, they didn't have a clue on what change and unity meant. These new jacks were gang oriented and held their own twisted philosophies. The young lions gradually pushed aside the older, wiser convicts. San Quentin became a breeding ground for senseless violence and racial wars with all of the attention focused on killing one another. The administration could now rest easy.

After doing fifteen years in San Quentin, Doc Holliday returned to the community to find there was no revolution to spearhead. The community seemed too centered around the dollar. Doc reluctantly gravitated towards his close friend Ray Ray Browning.

Ray Ray allegedly was operating a million dollar cocaine distribution ring that supplied parts of Pasadena, California and some sections in Los Angeles. When federal indictments came down Doc's name was on it. The two would both receive life sentences.

Doc could hold his own with anyone of the new jacks. A lot of youngsters sought advice and guidance from Doc in settling disputes. Doc was still physically fit for a man his age. I greeted Doc with open arms when I met him in the unit.

"Greetings, Doc. I heard a lot about you," I said showing respect for the older convict.

"I have anything you need as far as toiletries and snacks," I humbly offered.

"Pleased to meet you. Only thing I'm interested in right now is a cigarette. I've been on the plane all day," Doc said, his weary face turning into a smile.

"I don't smoke Doc. I'm sure I can get you some though," I said without much hesitation.

"Thanks, cool breeze," Doc replied with the satisfaction of meeting someone who was also from his hometown.

When imprisoned in another state where there are no homies you can feel alienated. When meeting homeboys who have a special character you will more than likely develop a close bond.

"Cool Breeze, you working out today?" Doc asks me.

"Yeah, Doc, let's go," I answered.

We'd come back from the yard that afternoon, Doc's arms swollen twice their size locking into an uncomfortable position from lifting weights.

"Hey, Cool Breeze, I can't move my arms," Doc says stretching his arms back and forth in an attempt to loosen them.

"Damn, Doc. How long has it been since you last worked out?" I asked.

"It's been a long time, Cool, since my San Quentin days," Doc said rubbing his aching arms.

"Doc, you're talking years, my man," I laughed.

◆ ◆ ◆

One late evening while we were mingling on the tier shooting the breeze, a Jamaican prisoner named Cee Lee approached us.

"Hey, California, you all want to use the phone?" he asked.

"What you mean?" Doc answered.

"I'll show you," Cee Lee said in a heavy laced Jamaican accent.

"Come keep watch," he said.

The staff's offices were on the bottom floor of the unit. The living area, beds and television room were down the range on the same floor. The guard's booth was upstairs on the upper floor where the guard usually sat most of the night censoring outgoing mail or reading porno magazines. The counselor's office was not occupied at night due to their schedule of day watch hours.

Lewisburg Federal Prison was old so the structure was outdated as far as security was concerned. The office had a wooden door with a small oblong window that was centered. The panes that held the glass in place were also wooden and held with old putty. Someone removed the putty so you could slide the glass out of the frame then stick your hand through the opening and turn the knob from the inside opening the door. Once inside you put the window back in place. No one ever knew you were inside.

After the 10:00 p.m. count most of the unit prisoners would be ready to call it a day. A dozen or so would stay up late hours watching television in the dayroom. What was so accommodating was that the dormitory style unit afforded prisoners the pleasure of never having to be locked in.

The unit guard would make his rounds at designated hours, but as long as we kept the light out, kept watch for one another, no one would ever know we were bilking the government phone. By dialing 9, the area code and your seven digit telephone number, we would call anywhere in the nation, courtesy Bureau of Prisons.

It was all good up until a point. One late evening Doc and I both were inside the counselor's office hidden behind the huge government desk dialing for dollars. Doc was on the phone, I was patiently waiting my turn, and inadvertently listening to his conversation for a sign he would wind it up, at the same time listening for the jingling of keys, a telltale sign that the unit guard was making rounds. Suddenly, I hear keys going inside the key hole.

I'll be damn. I'm thinking. I look at Doc, he look backs at me, then Doc quietly sets the phone back down before the door opens. The both of us are behind the desk like two squirrels hiding in a cubby hole. The light comes on, the guard walks to the front of the desk; he can't see us unless he gets behind the desk. If he does, we are busted.

The guard picks up the telephone and starts dialing. From under the desk all Doc and I see are the guards boots. Apparently the phone is ringing on the other end; he is unable to place his call. He walks back towards the door, cuts the light out, leaving. It was a close call.

"Doc, let's get out of here while we can," I said with a sigh of relief.

Doc responds nonchalantly, "He won't be coming back cool breeze, we alright."

We stayed up to 3:00 a.m. placing phone calls to girlfriends and relatives.

◆ ◆ ◆

Later during the week while I was in the dayroom watching television, Doc runs in out of breath and flops down in the seat beside me.

Sensing trouble, I thought Doc had killed someone or something.

"What's going on, Doc," I ask nervously.

Doc takes his shirt off handing it to me, he starts to answer but before he does guards rush in eyes darting around the dayroom.

One of the guards says, "It's him. The one there," he said pointing at Doc.

Doc looks at him like the guard has lost his mind for wrongfully accusing him. They escort Doc to segregation.

It would not be until at least two weeks before I learned what had actually happened that night; Doc sent me a message through someone coming from the hole. Apparently, Doc had been using the phone. We had used the phone so many times we became over confident and lax. We stopped watching for each other. Doc was caught slipping in the room by himself. He bolted past the guard, inadvertently knocking him off balance. This was why he ran into the dayroom breathing heavily. Initially, administrators believed that Doc had been trying to escape. But no bars were cut nor tampered with.

Doc sent a kite out to the yard asking me to come vouch for him at the DHO hearing. He asked me to be forthcoming about the events that had lead up to him being placed in the hole. Surely Doc would rather be sanctioned for illegal use of the telephone than to face charges for attempted escape.

During the investigation, SIS (an internal prison investigation by designated staff which consists of collecting information from snitches, prison files and other means) poured over Doc's state and federal prison files. What they discovered was that Doc was a former ranking Black Guerilla Family leader as well as a high level player in Ray Ray Browning's drug organization. Doc was cleared for the escape attempt but because of his high profile status, administrators transferred Doc to the nation's most secure federal prison—United States Prison in Marion, Illinois.

Meanwhile I concluded that dialing for dollars was not worth the risks.

After a few weeks in I-unit I was assigned to J-unit on the second floor. In J-unit there were Mafia bosses, a former union boss, and Herbie Sperling. Herbie had been allegedly operating a major heroin distribution ring in New York during the seventies, at one time supplying Nicky

Barnes, who later gave testimony against Herbie. Herbie was given life in prison.

I also met Buddy in J-unit. Buddy was from Baltimore, Maryland. We bonded instantly. On the entire Lewisburg compound there were only five of us from California. Confidence, Air Tight Slim, Kimbui, Pierre and me. There was a standing beef between D.C. boys and California cliques in the federal prison system, but our small numbers at Lewisburg made us less of a threat. There were over six hundred D.C. boys. They were busy feuding with the Baltimore cliques which was a carry over from the streets.

Our crew at Lewisburg gravitated around one another in the aggressive setting. We stood strong in the eyes of our enemies. We missed Doc's presence, but in the short time he was there he left us all with some of his wisdom.

"Doc is a good dude, a real stand up guy," I said to Kimbui, a homie from Oakland.

Kimbui's slave name was David Crane. He adopted the

Swahili name Kimbui as a way of denouncing his slave heritage.

"Yeah, I'm gonna miss the old man," Kimbui responded.

I smiled as I thought about the time we almost got busted using the telephone. Also walking the yard debating past and present issues.

The federal prison system is ominous. You can build a rapport with a friend in a prison be transferred and never see that individual again. The friendship Doc and I developed was cut short, it was one of mutual respect and appreciation. Ordinarily, trust in prison does not carry that far.

About a month or so later while on my way back from lifting weights in the hot, sunny, Pennsylvania heat I noticed a face peering from a window of the basement floor of K-Dorm, the holdover unit. I fixed my eyes to see who the face belonged to; I noticed the living quarters looked dark and damp. My initial reaction was one of disbelief that prisoners would have to sleep in such squalor.

I asked the young black prisoner, "Hey, are there any dudes down there from Cali?"

"Yeah, wait right here, you got a homeboy down here," he replied.

"Yeah, what's up homie?" a tall menacing looking convict appeared at the window.

"You from the house?" I asked.

"Yeah, cuzz, I'm from the coast, six-deuce."

I understood that the convict's allegiance was to 62nd Street Eastcoast Crip from Los Angeles, California. East Coast Crips is a conglomerate of individual Eastside Crip sets consolidated by Crip founder Raymond Washington shortly before his untimely death.

"I'm from Sixties," I responded

"I know some of your homies," Bub smiled.

"Righteous," I smiled.

Big Bub and a few other Crips had been caught up in Pennsylvania on drug distribution charges. Their arrest made local headlines which prompted the district attorney to make examples out of the Crips who exported cocaine to the state of Pennsylvania. The city of Los Angeles was already saturated with the powerful white powder for which the supply was greater than demand.

Work Call! Work Call, the P.A. system announced. At approximately 7:30 every morning prisoners who were assigned to work details filed out their housing units headed towards their respective work areas. Some prisoners worked food service, laundry, library etc., I carried my government boots every morning to the prison industries known as Unicor.

In the federal prison system most institutions have a factory which prisoners manufacture products for the federal government. Prisoner's wages for their labor range anywhere from twenty nine cents to one dollar per hour. A prisoner's pay may increase every sixty to ninety days, depending on his work performance.

After each eighteen month period of work, a prisoner is entitled to a longevity pay increase; this increase is ten cents per hour up until eighty-five months of continuous work.

Unicor, as a corporation, grosses billions of dollars yearly; there is no competition with a corporation who pays prison workers measly wages.

Unicor factories across the nation produce everything imaginable for the government. Lompoc factory builds electronic cables for the Department of Defense, Leavenworth has a textile factory, Oakdale facility in Louisiana produces institution clothing that are worn in all federal prisons for example, Khaki shirts and pants, tee-shirts, socks, and shorts.

There are a few call centers in some of the federal facilities also; Bureau of Prisons contracting through Unicor to do directory assistance for 500 companies such as Sprint and AT&T.

Despite low wages and long work hours, I enjoyed my work assignment in Unicor. The work kept me busy and before I knew it the day was over.

Working at the factory also enabled me to make money to be able to afford products sold at the commissary and call home regularly.

Most prisoners are not financially able to call home as often as their family would want to hear from them. The prison phone system requires a prisoner two choices: dial collect at an exorbitant rate (seven to nine dollars for every fifteen minutes) or dial direct at three dollars and forty-five cents for every fifteen minutes which is absorbed from the prisoner's account.

Either way, it is a financial strain on most families who are poor yet still trying to maintain family ties.

On August 22, 1989, I headed out to my prison job assignment at Unicor; I worked on an assembly line in the paint section of a metal factory. My co-worker was Naim from Philadelphia. We got along well. However, time plus misery causes anger in situations when least expected.

A prisoner has to acquire many faces to be able to adapt with the complexed personalities in a prison setting. To one you may be a listener, another, a lecturer, some others know nothing more than for you to beat them mercifully. It isn't until then that they concede that they are grateful for that understanding.

While working the assembly line that day, Naim and I began to disagree about whose turn it was to work the assembly line. Naim and I alternated in thirty minute shifts throughout the work shift. The disagreement quickly turned chaotic.

"Hey, Naim, it's your turn to run the line," I said watching the assembly line run without being monitored.

"Man, you must think I'm a zip fool if you think I'm going back up there to work again, it's your turn," Naim said with contempt.

"I just worked last, playboy; it's your shift," I reasoned.

Naim was trying to work me. The onlookers stopped production and began to gawk as Naim and I argued. He had gotten loud and out of control.

In a penitentiary environment where everything is mundane, the slightest deviation from the norm is enough to draw attention. Aware that an audience was watching us, Naim performed like an actor wearing stage make up.

"Yeah, nigga, I told you. I ain't doing shit, punk ass nigga!" Naim signified for the bored prisoners.

The words hit me like a dagger to the heart. Naim dissed me in front of other prisoners, which, by convict code, was not to go unchecked. If it went unchecked it would encourage other prisoners to also disrespect me one time or another. Not one to follow rigid rules that didn't make much sense to me anyway, I wanted to spare myself from responding foolishly so I opted to give Naim a way out.

"Man, what did you just say?"

"Nigga, you heard!" Naim said, "You are a punk!"

The statement fueled the fire that had already been ignited. I was trying to avoid putting Naim on the spot, but by doing so instead left him little opportunity to save face. Instead of a cunning and calculated reaction, I acted out of emotion; a mistake I would be mindful of in the future.

A steel pipe lay conveniently a few feet away in a pile of scrap metal. It was accessible in accommodating my response.

I'll show you who is the punk I thought while walking towards the pipe.

Naim had his eyes dead set on me as he back pedaled from the scene. Taking total advantage of his retreat and not wanting to let Naim out of my eyesight, I pursued after him with the pipe in my hand accelerating my speed. In the short run I closed the gap within striking distance of Naim. I swung the pipe, narrowly missing him. The next swing caught Naim on his upper back area. Naim let out a shrieking yelp running a few more paces. I pulled my arm back for a more effective strike but panicky Naim stopped quickly in his tracks causing me to collide into him. As I did Naim wrapped his arms around my body holding on for dear life preventing me from being able to swing the pipe again.

"Stop it man! Please stop," Naim pleaded.

"Why are you doing this to me?" he cried.

I struggled against his grip as he continued, "Somebody get this dude off me. I'm going home soon. You tripping man?"

Naim's will had been shattered to pieces. He'd broken before the fight had really got going. Until this point his words had been laced with venom, but the snake turned out to be a garden snake, looks like a rattler but when faced with opposition causes no harm. The prison deuces sounded off and the goon squad stormed in the building to restore order.

"Break it up!" the guards commanded as they rushed us wrestling the pipe out my hand, handcuffing me.

"Nigga, you ain't done nothing," Naim screamed now that he was safe.

I stared in disbelief. The nerve of this coward, I thought. That particular scenario forever taught me a lesson: All disrespect is not personal disrespect. Naim had no intention of backing up his words, that's all they were, empty words. If I had broken loose from the handcuffs he'd probably have pissed his pants. I glanced at the spectators while being escorted out of the factory. They got their chance to see what they were looking for. They will probably talk about this all week, I thought.

Again, I sat in the confines of segregation. I wondered what my future would hold. I'm never getting out of here, I thought, banging my fist against the concrete wall. The guy turned out to be a coward, bluffing for the crowd, pushing my buttons. I silently contemplated as I reviewed the incident in my mind. Then and there I vowed never again to allow anyone to have that much control over my actions. It made me feel vulnerable that I had reacted impulsively. I wanted to be able to suppress my anger and maintain control in these kinds of situations. Yet something sinister caused me to smile.

Who's the punk now, I thought.

After thirty days in isolation I was moved to the range of administrative segregation cells. My new cell was occupied by an elderly brother who had an oval shaped head sitting on a body with wide shoulders and barrel chest.

"What's up, young brother?" the convict said. He threw me off guard with his politeness.

"Ain't nothin," I shrugged, thinking a trap was being laid.

"What you in seg for?" he asked intending to engage in conversation.

"Rather not talk about it, brother," I said in an attempt to prevent the stranger from invading my mental space.

"It's cool. I understand brother. By the way they call me Big House," He extended his hand for an exchange of greetings.

"I'm Lacy," I said, shaking his hand. "What day do they exchange sheets, brother?" I asked fixing my bedding. I asked that particular question more so in an attempt to feed the conversation that was being forced on me.

"They change sheets on Thursday, my man. But you got to get up early because these crackers will sneak through and won't say anything," House said revealing his contempt for the guards.

I started feeling less leery about House as I opened up for dialogue.

Normally, under such conditions, blacks would react with

indifference to each other because of self hatred. Most black men from the East or Westcoast were indirectly affected by racism, so they were confused as to where the root of their hatred came from; most of the time that hatred was misdirected.

House, however, was from the (Old South). Experiencing racism firsthand in Mississippi gave House a unique perspective. House, a country boy, had been sent to Marion federal prison in the early eighties from the Mississippi state prison system for greater security needs. House experienced a new generation of racists while at the maximum security prison in Marion, Illinois. The Aryan Brotherhood, a white prison organization, whose members held a strong hatred for blacks and Jews, had murdered several black prisoners and two correctional officers in a short span.

The Aryan Brotherhood formed in 1964 in the California prison system at a time when racial conflicts between black, white and Chicano prisoners were on the rise. The Aryan Brotherhood, also known as The Brand, identified themselves by the numbers 666, the letters AB, or an Irish shamrock tatted on their bodies. To become a member one had to earn their bones, in other words kill an enemy of the Aryans. Once you became a member, you were in for life. Blood in; blood out.

Drug transactions, extortion and murder were routine for the Aryans. The running of the yard exemplified who controlled the flow of contraband and money inside the prison. It was common knowledge that in these prison settings white guards sometimes worked hand in hand with the Aryans in maintaining terror among the black convicts, by covertly supplying the Aryans with confiscated shanks and even street knives.

The Aryan Brotherhood code, "The enemy of my enemy, is my friend" strengthened unity between the Aryans and a diehard group of Southern California Mexicans, the Mexican Mafia, who also had a history of battling black convicts while inside California prisons.

Chapter 14 Aryan Brotherhood Reign of Terror

At the federal penitentiary in Marion, Illinois, the Aryan Brothers were on a constant course of violence with D.C. clique and other blacks. House related to me that he too collided head on with the Aryans while at Marion Prison. He got into an altercation with one of the younger cocky Aryan members on the weight pile over a weight bench, almost coming to blows. The young Aryan left the scene to solicit assistance from Aryan Jack, a Aryan hell raiser, who spewed his racist sentiments all over the prison compound. Aryan Jack and the young A.B. confronted House on the weight pile and threatened House.

"Check in nigger, you got to get off this line," Aryan Jack said walking off.

The confrontation infuriated House. Having been raised in the Deep South, House was subjected to racism all his life. House continued to pump weights until yard recall. He then consorted with a convict friend he had close association with while at Marion.

"I got into a beef with one of the Aryans and I need to take care of my business," the seething southern boy stated. "It's either him or me," he added.

The convict he spoke with didn't even need ask for further explanation, he knew in his heart that House had always been polite and never disrespected anyone. The convict then reached into his box of personal property pulling out his photo album. Sticking his finger and thumb in between the binding and pulled out a flat. A flat is a steel welding stock sharpened at both edges of one end to a point, creating a double-edge shank.

"Do you need assistance?" the convict asked as he handed House the weapon.

"Naw, man, all I want you to do is hold these for me," handing his friend a stack of family photos.

House then shook his friend's hand and left quickly, not wanting to involve the man with his course of action no more than he already had. Transporting the weapon in his waist band, House must have thought about all of the abuse that had been heaped upon him as a kid by the crackers in Mississippi.

"The nerve of this cracker" House said aloud as he approached the housing unit of the two Aryans.

As House entered the unit he saw Aryan Jack standing among a group of Aryans, calmly smoking a cigarette. Pulling out the shank, House walked towards the group with an accelerated pace, but before he reached them one of the Aryan members looked up saw House and broke and ran. The panic caused the others to flee also, including Aryan Jack.

House had one target in mind. That was Aryan Jack. Chasing the elusive Aryan up and down the tier was no easy task for House. When House would get close enough to Jack, Jack would grab hold of the railing that separates the second floor from the first floor and climb down. When House would climb down, Jack would elude House down another path. House continued his chase. He figured with a little more effort, he could get his man. Patience proved right. Jumping off the second tier, Jack hit the ground and lost his footing and buckled from fatigue. House, seizing the opportunity advanced and before Jack could continue to run, House pounced on top the Aryan, sticking the shank into his chest cavity again and again while administrators, who by now had run to the scene, yelled for House to stop.

"Come on House, that's enough, put the weapon down," pleaded one of the associate wardens.

It was not until Aryan Jack's body lay lifeless that House turned over his weapon to administrators crying uncontrollably.

"Damn you cracker! Why you make me do this," House admittedly cried.

The story was interrupted by the clanging of keys against the metal door.

"Chow time, gents; get your hot trays," the guard said.

As we ate House informed me that for the murder of Jack he plead to a ten year sentence to run concurrent with the life sentence he was already serving. Aryan Jack's prison file indicated that he had a violent temper and displayed aggressive behavior. It was also known that Jack threatened House at the weight pit, a threat that House took very seriously.

"Did the Aryans want to retaliate for you murdering Jack?" I asked.

"No," House answered.

"A lot of the Brotherhood members were relieved Jack was dead, but didn't openly say so. Jack kept the Aryans in a lot of beefs," House revealed as he put me up on the guerilla style attacks that had occurred at the maximum security prison that held some of the most dangerous convicts in the nation.

Three D.C. blacks and two correctional officers were killed during House's term in Marion Prison. House lays out the events for me in vivid detail which is legendary throughout the federal system.

The Aryan Brotherhood and D.C. blacks fought hard over control of the prison. One of the D.C. blacks, Charles "Steamboat" Stewart, had been murdered while in the control unit at Marion. The control unit was designed as a disciplinary quarters in which the most unmanageable prisoners in the feds were confined. The prisoners of control unit spent virtually twenty three hours locked in their cells. Bureau of Prison policy concerning the control unit was to break the aggressiveness of its prisoners housed there.

Steamboat, a documented booty bandit, harbored a hatred for the Aryans. Steamboat's dislike obviously must have grown intolerable. According to court records, on October 1, 1979, an Aryan member associate, Clayton Fountain, along with Hugh Colomb, signed a recreation log to recreate with Charles Stewart. Records indicate that each inmate agreed to this recreation session by their signature. The control unit guard had to have it approved by the senior officer. Later during a trial, the guard testified that he asked Charles Stewart if he was sure that he wanted to recreate with Fountain and Colomb.

The unit guard then proceeded to open all three cells simultaneously. Fountain and Colomb were the first out of their cells walking quickly to the front of the tier where Stewart's cell was. Stewart, wearing only a jockey strap, was surprised by Fountain as he lunged into the cell swinging a shank at Stewart. Stewart began to kick out at Fountain knocking him back out the cell. Stewart came out of the cell to fight his attackers which now involved Colomb. Fountain and Colomb in a tag team act stabbed and kicked Stewart while they attacked him. As Stewart was overcome, Fountain lay over his body stabbing him more that forty times screaming,

"Die bitch, die!"

Dragging Stewart's body down the range, guards looked on as Fountain taunted other black convicts who were in their cells. It was not until after Stewart had been killed that Fountain turned over his weapon to guards who were standing on the other side of the grill gate. Charles

"Steamboat" Stewart was reportedly stabbed over seventy times.

Two other murders that occurred in the control unit were that of Officer Clutts and Officer Hoffman. Clutts had been working the control unit and had a penchant for meticulously shaking down Tommy Silverstein's cell.

Silverstein was on the three man commission with two other Aryans, Edgar Hevle and Barry Mills, who oversaw the running of the Aryan Brotherhood in the federal system. Clutts had a hard-on for Tommy. The two had previously been in a pissing contest and Officer Clutts wanted to show Silverstein who was running things. Officer Clutts searched Silverstein's cell and confiscated some hobby craft painting materials and his mattress.

This infuriated Silverstein, who had had enough and wanted to even the score. A few days later Officer Clutts and two other guards escorted Silverstein to the showers. In the control unit it was procedure to handcuff any prisoner coming out his cell and for three officers to escort the prisoner. Silverstein lagged back to get something from fellow convict Randy Gometz, who was locked in his cell.

Silverstein stuck his handcuffed wrist through the bars of Gometz's cell, as he pulled his hands out much to the guard's surprise; Tommy Silverstein had one handcuff dangling from his wrist and a shank in his other hand. Silverstein charged at Clutts as the three guards fled towards the end of the tier to get behind the grill gate for safety. Clutts, however, did not make it. He slipped and fell near the shower area, Silverstein in a controlled rage stabbed Clutts fatally as his fellow officers who had locked themselves behind the grill gate looked on stunned.

In an ironic stage of events on the same day, hours later, on the other side of the control unit, Aryan associate Clay Fountain killed guard Hoffman while also on a three man escort to the showers. Fountain's reason, to keep tally with Aryan confederate Tommy Silverstein who had earlier committed his fourth murder. It was reported that after Fountain killed guard Hoffman, he jumped up and down as if he had just scored a touchdown.

Since the murder of the two guards in 1983, the entire prison remained on a permanent lockdown status keeping its prisoners confined to their cells twenty-three hours a day. No convict comes in contact with guards without being shackled hand and feet. In 1994, a new Marion style supermax prison Florence ADX in Colorado opened to house the nation's most dangerous prisoners. ADX was built specifically to house prisoners who required greater security needs.

Marion's long term prisoners were transported under heavy security to their new home in 1994. Tommy Silverstein spends twenty-four hours in a specially constructed cell underground in Leavenworth Prison since the murder of the guard, with no human contact. He was designated an unusual security policy of no human contact with anyone but prison staff.

After House's description of daily life and survival in Marion Prison I felt the need to lay on my bunk and go to sleep. I failed to find a rational reason how so much violence in such a secure environment went unchecked. How could Stewart be murdered so viciously? Where were the safeguards at the most secure prison in the nation? I imagined it to be an eerie and dangerous place.

Later in the week I went before a hearing officer to receive my sanctions for the assault on Naim. It was short and terse. Naim was allowed to go back to general population and I was given a separatee against him with a disciplinary transfer.

I had come back to the cell actually excited about the transfer. Since I left Lompoc for the stabbing I hadn't been near my family members. My relationship with them was distant. Their belief was that I was not trying to change my life.

People who have never experienced being in prison have no idea of the facets of daily prison life. There is a totally different set of rules among convict population.

With the transfer, House and I theorized that there were only three maximum security prisons; Lompoc, Leavenworth and Lewisburg. Atlanta penitentiary had been recently converted to a holding facility to detain Mariel Cubans while political talks on what the nation wanted to do with them continued. Terre Haute also a penitentiary was considering lowering its security, making me ineligible. So administrators would have to send me to the prison which I had not been to more recently. Lompoc, which sat off the California coast, seemed imminent.

"I'm not going to call my family until I get there. I'm going to surprise them," I said to House excitedly.

"Well, there it is there," House smiled.

I jumped on top of my bunk and thought about some friends wondering if they would still be there in Lompoc. Ironman, Milky and others I had developed close associations with. The following month I was summoned to Receiving and Departure.

"Lacy, let's go! Bring all your personal property. They want you at R&D, you're scheduled for the bus in the morning," the guard said.

It was the first good news I heard in years. I was so happy I wanted to shake the guard's hand for being the bearer of good news. Finally, I thought. Upon arrival to R&D my personal property was inventoried and packed.

"How many days will it take to get to California?" I asked.

The guard looked out at me over the top of his glasses and replied, "We are not scheduled to go to California."

"Then where am I going," I asked confused.

"According to my transfer list, you are being transferred to USP Marion, Illinois," the guard stated not showing any personal concern.

I heard it correctly, but it still had not registered. I wanted to inform the guard that there must have been some mistake. Yet, I knew otherwise. Nothing was a surprise to me anymore when it came to the Bureau of Prisons. I had been shipped around to three different states in less than four years. It felt like I had done more traveling than a three ring circus. Yet, traveling in the Bureau of Prisons was no laughing matter.

Normally I would have become defensive with the guard about the transfer, but I felt defeated. Losing was the hardest thing to accept at this point. It was because I fought so hard to retain my dignity and sanity in the face of the keepers. It was the only thing they hadn't been able to take from me so far. No one can get inside of you mentally unless you allow it.

When I returned to my cell from R&D, I no longer wore the devilish grin I had when I left it.

"What's happening, my man?" House asked concerned.

"Sending me to Marion," I replied curtly.

"What happened to Lompoc?" asked House.

"Don't know, don't care," I answered. "Forget these assholes."

"Marion is murderer's row, reserved for the most violent convicts," House said, still in disbelief.

No comforts could erase the image in my mind of Stewart and others who were murdered at Marion. It just wasn't safe there. In addition, the chatter and loud noise up and down the tier offered no solace to my mind. I had already traveled down the annals of my very worst fears.

Anticipating the worst, I thought about my future and could not actually see past Marion, paranoia would not allow it. In most prison settings where there are threats of real danger, it is hard for even the strongest to think beyond daily survival and maintain an optimistic outlook. Especially when death has no preference who it calls.

It is that fear of the unknown that creates anxiety which causes aggressive acts or total submissiveness in a brutal prison environment. That fear permeates every crevice of prison society in one form or another. Murder and assault reinforces the fear factor.

Chapter 15 Worst of the Worst- USP Marion

October 1989

The United States Penitentiary in Marion, Illinois held the nation's most violent, incorrigible prisoners.

J. Edgar Hoover once described it as a prison for the "Worst of the worst". Marion Federal Prison replaced Alcatraz Federal Prison which closed in 1963. Prisoner's who required close watch, escape artist, or those who were serious management problems in other prisons were sent there.

The average prisoner at Marion had either killed or escaped at one time. The Bureau of Prisons had contracts with state prisons in the nation to house high profile prisoners in Marion as a measure to have greater control over that prisoner. New Afrikans Sekou Odinga and Sundiata Acoli were sent there. Among Marion's other elite were mob boss (John Gotti), Israeli spy (Jonathan Pollard), Columbian Cartel (Carlos Lehder) and others. No prisoners in the Bureau of Prisons were watched closer than the prisoners at Marion. The minimum stay is three years. A convict must spend twenty-three and one half hours confined to his cell. When a prisoner arrives at Marion he goes through a process over a number of years designed to break his will.

Each year a prisoner appears before a unit review to determine if he is ready to advance to the next phase of the three year program. For example, at your first annual hearing, if the unit committee were not satisfied with your adjustment, the committee members would not advance you to the next phase of the program. What this means is that what is supposed to be a three year program could potentially turn into six, seven or eight years until administrators deemed the prisoner programmable again.

The prison bus rested its brakes in front of a modern style penitentiary, which looked like a college campus with a manicured lawn and frosted glass windows on the administration building. Yet the human warehouse was far from its illusionary structure. The ride to Marion Federal Prison from Pennsylvania had taken thirteen grueling hours and I was wearing the black box. The "black box", a small square metal box that fits over your handcuffs and is locked with a key, is supposed to prevent prisoners from picking the lock on the handcuffs during transit or to restrict movement of prisoner's hands who may become assaultive. Houdini himself may have had difficulty freeing himself. During this arduous trip, the images of the murders that occurred in Marion etched themselves in my mind.

As the prisoners shifted in their seats, a phalanx of guards converged towards the bus, each prisoner was escorted off the bus one by one by baton wielding guards.

Thirteen prisoners wearing shackles and waist chains were lined up outside the administration building and thirteen guards escorted each of us to Receiving and Departure. The presence of force was a subtle indoctrination to show prisoners who were in control. We sat in R&D for over an hour while being admitted into the prison. Taken separately into adjoining rooms, we were questioned.

"Do you have any separatees?"

"Are you gang affiliated?"

"What are you here for?"

After the counselor concluded his shoot from the hip question session he told me that I would be assigned to D-Unit. I was then taken back to the holding tank where curious prisoners asked,

"What did they say to you?"

"What unit are you going to?"

"They're putting me in D-Unit," I answered "D-Unit?" a convict on his second tour of Marion echoed back.

"D-Unit is a gang unit, it's where the Aryans, Mexican Mafia, D.C. clique and other gangs are housed," the con said, startling me with his unsolicited information.

"Thanks a lot, my man, but I have no choice in the matter," I responded in a gruff tone.

"Lacy, up front, let's go," the escort guard commanded while fondling the handcuffs as if he received sexual gratification from using them.

The walk down the long empty corridor felt like walking the last mile. All I seemed to be thinking of was how clean the meticulously waxed corridor floors were. Catching a glimpse out of one of the windows, I took notice of the glimmering sun bouncing off the panoramic view over the hills.

What a way to waste your life, I realized for the umpteenth time. As the guard escorted me inside the foyer of D-Unit, the atmosphere seemed dour and quiet. An eeriness crept over me like I had stepped into a morgue. Not a lot of whooping and shouting like other prisons I'd been to. A deadly silence filled the air.

As I was escorted to the upper tier on D range I shuffled past the first cell and took a mental note of the convict I glanced at out of my peripheral view. It was the coal black face of Terry Trice-El, he was a D.C. clique leader. Trice-El had picked up a couple of murders during his confinement and was involved in countless stabbings.

Administrators labeled Trice-El as a predatory prisoner among any population he was in.

"What's up Cali?" he shouted as he recognized me.

We were familiar with one another from the federal penitentiary in

Lompoc, California where I had first met Terry. Trice-El held no animosity towards California cliques.

He did not discriminate who he beefed with and was known to power play within his own rank.

"What's up?" I nodded my head upward signifying that I welcomed his greeting.

Convicts upon entering unfamiliar prison settings generally consume the atmosphere before engaging meaningless dialogue. The greeting would be sufficient until we had an opportunity to engage in unmonitored conversation.

Further down the range was Chief Malik. Malik formerly known as Jeff Fort is the founder of the Black P. Stones of Chicago. Years later he converted his organization to function with Moorish Science Temple calling themselves "El Rukns" translated as "The Stone" in Arabic. The federal government firmly believes that Jeff Fort had ties with former Lybian president Muammar Gaddafi.

In D-Unit there were also a high ranking cadre of Aryan Brotherhood; Barry Mills, Edgar Helve, T.D. Bingham, who were appointed commissioners for the Brand. Tommy Silverstein was no longer commissioner due to him being held incommunicado.

Mexican Mafia members Champ, Black Bobby, Ronnie Bruscino and Bosco were there, too.

John Gotti of the Gambino Family and Nicky Scarfo of the Philadelphia mob were also D-Unit residents. Another unfamiliar figure on the range with a familiar actor son was James Harrelson.

The government contends that James Harrelson, on a contract killing, murdered a federal judge over thirty years ago. Given a life sentence and sent to Marion, his son, Woody Harrelson who starred in the sitcom "Cheers" as well as several motion picture movies, "White men can't jump" with Wesley Snipes, visits his dad regularly.

The guard stood at the end of the tier manipulating the automatic control panel opening the door in which would be my living quarters for at least a year.

"Step inside," the guard shouted down the range.

Brrrmmm, bammm! the cell door slammed behind me. The cell was cold and empty. As I glared around the room, I noticed a concrete platform eighteen inches high and six feet long, it was my bed. Also in the tiny room in the corner was a stainless steel toilet connected with a sink. The entire size of the cell was that of a very small bathroom in a home.

To keep one from going stir crazy, administrators provided each cell with a thirteen inch black and white television. Some Marion Prisoners would spend all day fixated on the tube. We were allowed outside recreation once a week for a two hour session. The rest of the rec days were one hour inside on the tier. Inside rec consisted of nine prisoners at a time, which sometimes either began or ended with a session of fisticuffs or in some cases death. Meals were served through a tray slot cut into the cell door.

As stated previously, Marion was designed to break the convicts will and deprive him of unmonitored movements that exist in normal prison settings, to curtail the prisoner's predatory or aggressive behavior.

There were a lot of psychological games played by the administration at Marion to keep the prisoners in a constant state of confusion. Prisoners' letters were held intentionally for long periods of time, outgoing letters were mysteriously lost. Other psychological tactics were middle of the night shakedowns. Convicts awakened, handcuffed and moved out the cell while guards literally scattered the prisoner's property about the cell—boot print marks of the guards left on family pictures or bed sheets to provoke anger.

Marion convicts were only allowed two ten minute phone calls per month, which stifled any family support that prisoner may have had previously to arriving at Marion. Fighting the oppressive and torrid summer heat inside the hot 9x6 cell with no relief except for the government issued white towel held under tap water and applied ceremoniously to the face. Discomfort after discomfort affected one's sanity and willpower. Some endure and become stronger, some fail to draw from their God given inner strength and falter under pressure. None go unaffected by the demented mind games played out in Marion Prison. It will either make you or break you.

I sat on the green plastic hospital style mattress that laid flat on top of the cement slab, the kind that makes you sweat during the night because of your body heat. I watched a bug move freely outside of the cell, the roach has more freedom than I do, I thought.

I did not have a bedroll yet so a guard interrupted my thoughts,

"Lacy here's your bedroll," he said stuffing it through the tray slot.

"Well, that's room service for you," I remarked.

The guard not in a mood to match wits just smirked, knowing he would not tolerate my verbal sarcasm.

"You'll get a television in just a bit," he said. Although television viewing filled a lot of the void, watching it day in and day out became monotonous in itself. There is no mental stimulation involved in TV watching. Many prisoners spend countless hours being hypnotized by the one eyed monster when it is more advantageous to read or tune into one's own thoughts becoming contemplative of self.

When it's you and those four walls you have no choice but to take a look at yourself. A lot of times you will not like what you see, but that's what growth and change is all about, battling the demons inside, taking responsibility for your actions and the past. Becoming a wiser and more responsible person.

For the first time I interacted positively with my subconscious. Doing so, facilitated a desire for growth and change over the next few years while confined to the 9'x6' cell in solitary. I tried to spend every waking or sleeping hour preoccupied with as much cognitive mental functioning as possible for fear that if there were any void insanity might creep in and destroy me. It was my biggest fear.

My daily activities started with a 6:00 a.m. wake up to eat the breakfast tray that was shoved through the tray slot. At times it made you feel like you were a caged animal, but you learn to look past and focus on a bigger picture.

After breakfast I watched the early morning news until 7:30. I would turn off my TV and begin a morning study of psychology, economics, philosophy and various other scholastic readings. It was during those morning hours I found my brain more receptive to learning.

By 9:30 after two and one half hours of intense study I would roll up my mattress and begin a calisthenics routine that consisted of burpies, push-ups, sit-ups, jumping jacks, etc. Upon completion of the workout I'd take a birdbath until I was unlocked for showers. Showers were afforded with your recreation period on the tier. Every day before the birdbath, I spent time on cell maintenance. Wipe the floor down with a soapy towel, clean sink and commode, wipe walls.

Noon the lunch trays were served. After lunch I started back on my assignments from a college correspondence course I enrolled in, learning to read Spanish. I also used this time to write or respond to mail I received during the week.

Those studies would go on until 4:00p.m. near the institutional mandatory count. I would tune into a couple of local news programs then World News Tonight with Tom Brokaw.

It would not be until after my mind had been utilized for extended periods of learning that I would relax and watch various sitcoms and entertainment programs until 11:30 p.m. By choice. I'd turn off the small box and retreat to a world of dreams or nightmares, whichever would carry me through the night. Even then while sleeping, I would grow, interpreting my dreams or nightmares trying to decipher their meanings as learning experiences.

During the sleepless nights in Marion Prison, I internally tried to sort out the confusion about my childhood. I would mentally revisit my past, replaying chain of events that occurred, looking for answers. I would analyze frame-by-frame what had created my self-destructive mentality. Why? I asked myself.

Through examining patterns of my past destructive behavior and comparing with the present, I concluded that often during my young life I had seemed to continually repeat poor choices over and over again to the point of even in adult hood having no concrete sense of direction.

Whenever I failed it was easy to shift the blame, using the age old excuse of my parents not providing me with a stable home environment as a child, as opposed to facing the truth that I was the only person responsible for my foolish actions. As I sat in the bleak and grim cell, I knew that I could not go on living that lie. I was the only one who could change my thinking and behavior from counterproductive to productive.

Failure to deal with one's emotional past only causes misery and detachment which in turn leads to anger and aggression. At times we are so consumed in life's struggles that we don't take time to reflect on our past in order to gauge our future. Without doing so we never learn who we are or where we are going. We tend to surge aimlessly through life wearing blinders, moving about haphazardly.

These were the seeds of thought that through time formulated in me a strong desire for change. On another note, the three years in isolation challenged my perspective on life in general. I grew tired of finding myself in the same rut, spinning my wheels, never moving forward. The abnormal periods of isolation had a sobering effect on my mind. For the first time my mind started to evolve. Yet my past haunted me night after night and on many occasions I awoke miserable from the nightmares of a torn past and sweaty from the green plastic mattress.

The loneliness of isolation became challenging. With a burning desire to stay connected with the outside world I submitted my name and register number to be added to the pen pal section of the magazine (Black Romance), a monthly tabloid featuring love stories. There were several responses to my ad that read:

"Black man, 29, incarcerated and lonely. Incurable romantic, seeking correspondence with female. Race not important."

Several women responded to my ad, I developed a rapport with a young woman from Chicago. Linda came forth humorous and natural.

"I weigh 400 pounds," she joked in one of her first letters.

Greeting me with, "Hey knucklehead." A warm, trusting friendship ensued. The woman took a chance on me applying for a visit.

"I can hardly wait to see you, Linda, but I must warn you, I also weigh 400 pounds (smile)."

Although prisoners at Marion Prison visit behind thick Plexiglass windows while communicating on telephones, it did not discourage us from getting to know each other and enjoying one another's company.

"I thought you weighed 400 pounds," I remarked while lusciously gazing into her hazel eyes.

Linda wore no makeup; her smooth clear skin was highlighted by the raspberry lip gloss that accentuated her natural beauty.

"I see you don't weigh 400 pounds either," she smiled approvingly.

Her eyes roamed my body that had been fine tuned from rigorous calisthenics and daily exercise. We talked the entire visit, laughing and sharing intimacies. Although the penitentiary is not the most desirable setting for romance there are a significant percentage of women who prefer to meet a mate who is incarcerated for friendship or romance.

Those women compare relationships with that of men who are not incarcerated and conclude that some men in prison are far more attentive to stimulating a woman's emotional needs, where as free men are more in need of a sexual relationship. Occasionally, Linda would return to visit me and our friendship grew with time. When people are honest and real in relationships they build on foundations of trust. Those friendships usually weather the storm.

During the three year isolation program at Marion Prison I reflected on a lot of my past which helped me change and transform mentally. My term of isolation in Marion Prison was nearing its end. I appeared before a final review to determine if I had satisfied the requirements to be transferred to another prison with more freedom of movement in an open population.

The unit committee had been monitoring my progress as they do each prisoner and over the past three years assessed my conduct determining that I could function in a normal prison setting. I'd finally been recommended a transfer to Lompoc, California. If anyone has served a long term isolation program they'd probably concede that getting released from that program after a extended period of isolation is a tremendous burden lifted.

I wanted to reunite with my mom. I was equipped with a new understanding and self awareness. I now understood the circumstances of our past. I realized that she was the victim of domestic abuse and it inhibited her from having any real control inside the Adams home.

The transfer also meant I would be eligible for a parole hearing. In Marion Prison no prisoner sees the parole board until he transfers from there. It just doesn't happen. But, with my record clean for the past three years, parole seemed hopeful for the future.

Chapter 16 Lompoc Revisited

The year was 1992, there had been a war on drugs starting in 1987, and the federal prison system that once had been reserved for white collar crimes, high level drug distributors and bank robbers were now swarming with street crack dealers and young gang bangers. Many who were unfocused and bitter. A lot of them were given Draconian sentences ranging from ten, twenty, thirty years for small amounts of crack cocaine. Majority of them never have spent a day of their life in prison.

As we walked through the corridor of Lompoc carrying bedrolls unshaven and unkempt due to several weeks in transit, I noticed three young men posturing in the shadow of the control center wearing sagging pants mad dogging us with intimidating stares. Neither of them looked over twenty one. They hadn't a clue to the seriousness of their predicament. I could read through their exterior mask: Fear and confusion. I saw myself seven years ago looking at the youngster's. I understood their existence. I could relate to their confusion.

Intentionally averting their stares I kept focused on the sporadic activity of the other prisoners in the corridor, seeing if I could recognize any old friends.

A lot of new bootys, I thought.

Lompoc had changed a great deal since the last time I was there. Drugs and prison brew were rampant. Several murders had occurred in a short period of time. At least four in one year. One set of circumstances in particular produced three deaths. There was a knifing in front of L-Unit between Pacific Islanders and whites. Two prisoners were lying in pools of blood fatally wounded before the staff had a chance to respond. The deuces sounded off. The first staff member to respond was one of the paint shop supervisor's, upon reaching the scene of blood and gore he had a massive heart attack and died right on the spot where the attacks had taken place. I doubt if we were even locked down for a day.

Another killing happened in J-Unit, where I was housed. A white, who was allegedly dealing drugs, refused to kick in to the Aryan Brotherhood. He slept in late one morning and was murdered a couple hours before lunch. The business of the day went on as usual. Killings were just a momentary inconvenience to the prisoners of Lompoc population. No one seemed to even be concerned.

In 1993 Mutula Shakur, former Black Panther member, arranged a concert to be held in Lompoc Prison auditorium, coinciding with black history month. His step son, rapper Tupac Amaru Shakur with Thug Life, and rapper Yo-Yo were scheduled to attend as guest of the African Cultural Society, a prison based cultural group, with Mutula as chairman.

Mutula requested a security detail from the population of Crips, Bloods and 415 Bay Area to protect Tupac and Yo-Yo in the event anyone thought of bringing harm to the guest of the African Cultural Society. I was fortunate to have been part of that security detail. Although Yo-Yo was not able to make it, Tupac showed us love with his encore performance, blasting the system with his anti-police lyrics, performing several original rap beats. Tupac Amaru Shakur, the young fiery rapper, uplifted our spirits that day. May he rest in peace. Yo-Yo did show in another performance at Lompoc auditorium the next year which ended in a riot between Crip and Blood members. Yo-Yo was safely escorted out. I was not in attendance due to having already been transferred from the prison.

While I was at Lompoc I made goals to continue my education (college classes), completing a business computer course, which would prepare me for a hearing with the parole board for the first time since I had been locked up for the postal robbery. I felt that since I was showing some progress the parole board members would overlook the aggressions of my past.

Yet, the surrounding negativity of the prison environment pulled at me from all sides. There were no assurances of parole without the imminent threat of drama rising from the pores of Lompoc prison.

In J-Unit, any day was subject to bring drama. A young gang member going by the name Boo Rock, from forties Neighborhood Crip, and a convict from Detroit, named Cowboy, were playing dozens with each other and it got out of control.

Threats were exchanged. Cowboy taking it seriously ended up

chasing Boo Rock around the unit with a shank. Boo Rock not taking any chances at getting any holes poked in him and being the quicker of the two got away. The conflict caused a situation between the Crip faction who were a few hundred deep, against convicts from the Eastcoast supporting Cowboy.

Some crip elders wanted to keep the situation isolated to the unit to prevent an unnecessary full scale battle. Besides, we were on our home turf. The decision was for Boo Rock to handle his beef. Him and Cowboy would butt heads, with knives or fist, without any outside interference. Since I was an elder in J-Unit where the conflict occurred I was called upon to mediate the dispute, meaning someone had to go.

"You got to put your work in homie; it's your beef plain and simple. Win, lose or draw. We're not trying to involve everyone in a situation you can avoid," I explained to Boo Rock.

The homies wanted to also discipline Twin, a young homie from the same neighborhood as Boo Rock. He was there on the scene when Cowboy chased Boo Rock. He failed to assist his homie.

The witch hunt against Twin had been secretly brewing and news of it reached Little James, an original Westside Crip, from 118 Eastcoast. While sitting at the tables at the chow line, Little James spoke, "Warlock, I hope no one is planning on disciplining Twin," he shot at me.

"Naw, Homie, that ain't going down like that," I responded.

I agreed with Little James for the same reasons. Twin, first was not a Crip. He had no expectations from anyone in that regard. Secondly, Twin did not understand prison protocol, never having been to prison; simply he was not cut out for what others had expected of him. He was given a pass.

Boo Rock, on the other hand, was a seasoned gang banger, was actively participating as a Crip, had attended several meetings where combat readiness had recently been an issue and knew what he was expected to do.

Needless to say, the rallying cry was combat readiness. If Boo Rock did not retaliate, it would send a message to others that aggression towards the Crip car would go unchallenged. If a homie puts himself in a position by playing the cards, then he must accept the hand he is dealt.

It was up to me to delegate to the younger homies what action to take. After repeated persuasions for Boo Rock to retaliate, he adamantly refused.

"I don't want no trouble homie, I'm cool on that!" Boo Rock insisted.

"Fool, you wasn't cool on it the other day when you were throwing up your set, nigga, we ain't fakin' around here, get busy or check in," Tiny C Dogg threatened before he stormed off.

Boo Rock faced a dilemma that was like a double edged sword.

Damned if you do damned if you don't. I approached Boo Rock again one on one in an attempt to help him understand the confusion he had caused himself. I'd rather see him go away than to face the unavoidable wrath of the homies. Yet, at the same time trying to help Boo Rock toward a peaceful solution could be detrimental to me.

"Look homie, I don't care, one way or another, what you do. The choice is yours. But, man to man, you gotta pay the piper. You were fully aware of what you were mandated to do. It would be in your best interest to put your work in or do the honorable thing and check yourself in."

"I'm not checking in anywhere, if the homies want to deal with me then let's do it!" Boo Rock blurted out foolishly, lacing up his government boots.

It's amazing how twisted peoples thinking can be at times. Here, Boo Rock lacked the courage to protect himself when he needed to, but he's ready to fight a bloody battle with his own ranks.

The young lion homies beat Boo Rock senseless in the TV room administering boot therapy. They sent him away lumped up, dazed and confused. I slept uneasy that night. Here I am involving myself in the very same situations that kept me in so much trouble. I'm getting too old for this nonsense I rationalized.

However, at times in order for good things to manifest, unfavorable must take place. Twin was spared, hoping have learned a valuable lesson. Perhaps Boo Rock experienced one as well. Anytime I could give advice to the youngsters to deter aggression and conflict I would do so.

I'd walk the yard with a few youngsters, one on one, sharing my insightful knowledge and experiences which generally consisted of tapping into ones common sense and persuading that individual to learn how to use it. I gave invaluable lessons to Miles from Lantana Block, Bear from Nine-0 and Sniper from Rolling Sixties to name a few.

"Homie, you are in a fight every time I look around, that's crazy," I said to the big youngster known as Miles.

"Cuz, these dudes be trippin," Miles shot back.

"See that's the problem Miles, forget these dudes. Do your thing. Focus on Miles and I promise you these dudes won't even exist in your mind. It's real simple," I advised.

"You right, homie," Miles replied.

Miles fought again in less than a week. There seems to be no gauge when change may occur in others or for that matter self. Some change overnight, others never do, growing into old fools. Miles was basically a good youngster at heart but was not wise enough to understand that all disputes don't necessarily have to be settled with hands. Through learning and understanding my own past, I developed enough patience to motivate the youngsters to try and think wisely.

Although the road ahead still proved difficult in terms of empowering myself with positive reminders of change, I had made a valuable transition in the past four years learning to control my anger and aggression which had caused problems for me in the past. It was quite an experience spending the better part of my life living inside the hell I created. Good things started happening for me after experiencing so many hardships over the past seven years. My case manager summoned me to her office one morning for Unit Team Review. The Unit Team consists of a prisoner's case manager, counselor and unit manager.

"Mr. Lacy, have a seat," Ms. Macias spoke while looking into her computer.

"This is your yearly review. I see you have completed several courses since you have been here at Lompoc and staying out of trouble," she said.

"Well, your custody points have dropped to medium security. Do you want me to put you in for transfer or would you like to stay here?" she swiveled her chair around facing me.

Actually, I never imagined that after leaving the most secure prison in the nation (Marion), that I would be eligible for a reduction in custody so soon.

"Ms. Macias, the only transfer that I would accept right now is closer to home. I've spent too many years away from my family to go anywhere further," I reasoned.

Ms. Macias studied me closely.

"So I was thinking a transfer to Terminal Island," I pitched.

"There is no guarantee you will get it but I will recommend Terminal Island."

"Thanks, Ms. Macias."

I smiled as I thought about the different incidents that I had been through over the years. I thought about those whose lives ended inside the beast suddenly and violently. Some higher power had definitely been watching over me.

Chapter 17 Club Fed 1993

There is a quote that goes something like, "All's well that ends well."

I could relate to that saying at this point the way everything fell in place. I was at my lowest point for so long that any progress in terms of moving foward were considered blessings to me.

Terminal Island was like club fed. It was situated five minutes from Long Beach, twenty minutes from Compton and thirty minutes from South Central, Los Angeles. It was ideal for visiting. You could not get any closer. It literally sat right on the Pacific Ocean. Three parts on the water, one part land. While on the recreation yard jogging around track you could look right past the barbed wire fence directly into the Ocean.

Yachts and small boats sailed by all day, occasionally women on some of the boats would bear their breast to prisoners recreating on the yard as the prisoners made cat calls.

T.I. had tennis courts, a bocce ball court, softball field and weightlifting area. The weather was what one would expect of sunny California.

The cafe style kitchen reminded you of dining in a restaurant; salt and pepper shakers on every table with napkin holders. Some of the living quarters were dormitory style; others were two-man rooms.

Most prisoners who were sent to Terminal Island maintained clear conduct; the slightest infraction could get you sent out of the facility. T.I. was ideal for someone who was trying to program. The yard was at peace. No riots, stabbings, killings.

In the relaxed environment I could set new goals and formulate ideas appropriate for change. Although I could not change the circumstances of my past, I could be responsible for my future. After a couple months in T.I., I was scheduled for a parole hearing.

The United States Parole Commission was to meet at the institution in December 1993. Armed with a brown legal folder full of certificates of achievement from several continuing education programs, my G.E.D., college course credits, several letters from family members, friends, and good work reports, I appeared before the parole board optimistic about getting a date.

The parole examiners screened my prison files, probing me about my plans for the future, also wanting to see if I showed remorse for the crimes I committed. The parole examiners asked me to step out the room so they could render a decision, I complied.

As I sat outside the room awaiting my fate I pondered the variables in regards to the hearing. My anxiety level rocketed. The parole examiners could continue me to my expiration date which was an additional twelve more years, the examiners could deny parole leaving me in limbo until deemed parolable (I could re-apply every two years), a date could be set anywhere in between my one-third eligibility date and two-thirds date, or immediate release was an option being that I had already satisfied one third of my sentence.

Thinking of these possibilities drained me. My life was literally in the hands of men who had what was considered the "God" complex.

I was summoned back before the panel of parole examiners.

"Mr. Lacy, obviously you are not the same person who entered prison a decade ago. You have done quite well in the past few years. The parole commission will move at this time to grant parole for December 1996. We will send a notice of final action in twenty days. Continue the good programming," one of the examiners remarked.

"Thank You," I replied.

The parole meeting was adjourned. Although it was not an immediate release, I could be out in under three years. It was something to be thankful for considering my history of violence during my incarceration. I could now bring closure to the events that led me to prison and start my life over.

I felt relief for the first time in a decade. I was standing at the end of a long tunnel where for many years there was no end in sight—only hopelessness and despair.

Until now, my future had been clouded with uncertainty. My last years in prison were disciplinary free. I had started reaping rewards versus bitter conflict.

Opportunity had blessed me with two women at a time when I felt female companionship was desired more than ever. Leah, was a Christian, and lead singer of a church choir which consisted of six women with beautiful voices. The pastor of their church and the choir attended services at Terminal Island prison once a month to deliver a sermon as well as sing.

I sat front row when these women performed because they were very good singers and I noticed the slim dark skin singer hold several glances whenever she would look my way. Never had I seen jet black complexion on a woman yet so smooth. Her smile was also radiating. After a few encounters watching this woman watch me I felt compelled to make a move. The next time they were scheduled to attend our services I would have my name and prison number already written on a piece of paper and slip it to her. God forbid if the Pastor happened to witness it.

Leah sung again at the next service. When services ended some members of the audience were individually thanking the choir members and Pastor for their visit with us.

Leah had her back to me as I approached. She had just finished giving hugs to eager men in search of a magic touch from someone in the outside world that would perhaps free themselves of the loneliness they were presently faced with.

So was I, but to be honest, I was not looking for an act from God.

"Excuse me Miss," I said softly, holding my arms out gesturing for my hug also.

I embraced this woman with firmness yet comforting.

Not too long that would attract prying eyes.

"I think you have a beautiful voice, I enjoy hearing you sing. You lift my spirits every time I see you," I added. It was of course true.

"Thank you," she responded.

"I'm James," I offered my hand for a greeting.

"Leah," she put her soft hand in mine. As she cupped my hand, she felt the slip of paper I was holding between my fingers.

Before she could think I spoke.

"I hope I'm not out of line in anyway, but I was wondering if you could take my name and number. I would really like to correspond with you," I said with eyes of a small puppy.

Leah took the paper just as fast as I handed it to her. "If the Lord allows me time to, I will write you a letter," she responded.

I couldn't ask for anything more.

It had been a little over a month before I would receive a letter from

Leah. Actually I was not expecting to hear from her, so I was kinda taken by surprise. The correspondence was cordial; there were several references to Biblical scriptures. I knew very little about the Bible so it took a lot of effort researching the New King James' Version in order to be on the same page with her.

My letters were well scripted and charming. I've always had a knack for writing. I learned as much about Leah as she was willing to tell me. Leah aspired to pursue a career in music. She would have been very successful as a singer had someone given her that opportunity. Her voice was dynamic, she was a natural.

The more Leah became comfortable with me, she opened up her heart. Letters were no longer enough. Leah filled out and mailed a visiting application requesting to see me. It was approved. Every Friday Leah and I spent hours in the visiting room wrapped in each other's embrace.

I would not officially say we were in a relationship; nor was it love. But we consumed each other's thoughts day in, day out. Within the year of this fleeting romance we were faced with a dilemma. There was a conflict between Leah visiting me, and coming to the institution as a contract visitor with the church choir. Because of this oversight, Leah would no longer be able to visit me. Rules and regulations would not allow it. Leah decided that she could do God's work better among the inmate population rather than try to swim upstream to hold on to romance.

Michelle was a different situation. We were hooked up by a mutual friend, Anita. Michelle watched NCAA basketball games with enthusiasm, liked to write and talked on the phone religiously. She was pecan-brown complected, 5 foot four, and busty.

Michelle had to have her bras custom-made. Michelle and I became intimate through time and she visited whenever she could be there. If there anything that a man wants more after spending a great deal of time in prison, is a good woman to love and cherish when he comes home. Michelle was willing to ride it out to the end.

If you ask anyone who has ever been to prison, they would concede that any day is subject to failure. Just when you think you have everything figured out, all of the variables that are constantly working against anything good in the prison environment come to fruition.

In the penitentiary you will find prisoners squabbling over almost anything. Because administrators control nearly everything a prisoner does while confined, prisoners attempt to validate their own autonomy by trying to control some aspects of the prison environment where the prisoners themselves must exist.

A youngster, twice my size, had no respect for personal codes that had been implemented among the convicts in the unit I was in to reserve seating space in the television room. Convicts marked their chairs so there would be no confusion over who the chair belonged to. For example, a chair may be marked (Joe), (213) indicating a area code in Los Angeles, or (New York).

This particular youngster had his feet propped up in my chair which was unattended at the time. I noticed it as I casually walked into the TV room. I scanned the room; there were no other chairs available but my own which was being used as a footstool. I approached the youngster respectfully.

"Excuse me, man, let me get that chair from you."

"I'm using it, man," he responded, his face revealing agitation.

I then attempted to use calm as a weapon to get an understanding, "Say, brother, you're using it for your feet. Besides, it's my chair."

"I ain't your brother and not trying to hear all that dumb shit about a government ass chair," his face now twisting into an ugly mask.

Kindness never works with idiots. I tensed as fear overwhelmed me. It wasn't fear of the youngster, but what my next reaction may be.

By now I had learned the dynamics of prison culture well. If you are thinking of doing harm to someone, you may as well think clearly about what you are getting yourself into.

With this in mind I retreated, my head clouded with anger and confusion. I was still a reactionary when it came to dealing with anger, albeit a more dangerous one. But all I could think of was how polite I tried to be, but was totally dissed.

Ironically, I sought out one of the youngsters I had been lecturing on how to keep a low profile.

"Homie, let me use your strap," I said referring to a prison made shank.

"What up big homie, you aight?" Uukay asked concerned.

"Yeah, I'm straight. Just let me get that," I answered clearly irritated.

The issue wasn't about the chair anymore. It was about the exchange of words that had taken place. I felt totally disrespected.

The youngster hadn't even noticed me; by the time he looked up I was already closing the door and was inside his room. I wore a jacket to conceal the shank I carried in case we could not come to an understanding.

"My man, I need to holla at you for a minute," I said with a chill calm.

He looked up at me startled and apparently frightened.

"I left the dayroom without an apology from your foul-ass mouth," I said searching his eyes for weakness.

"I…I apologize, man, no disrespect meant," he finally said nervously offering his humblest apology.

"I'm telling you one time and one time only fool, don't ever disrespect me again," I added as insult to injury.

I did so intentionally to crush the young man's ego so that he could not feel that he got out on me verbally. I really did not care what anyone else thought. It is unfortunate that some inmates are constantly disrespectful and if you confront them about it they will become defensive. It's like a jungle in prison where only the strong survive, if you are humble and meek it only signifies weakness from people who do not understand humility or the value of respect. It seems as if the only understanding they come to know is through violence.

Some prisoners become anti-social to prevent being drawn into the madness that exists inside the prison setting. Prisoners usually with longer sentences eventually succumb adopting prison codes necessary for survival that would be considered abnormal in society.

I felt relieved that I was able to bring about an understanding without having to result to physical aggression. Another lesson learned that all disrespect should not be taken personal. It was a close call.

Chapter 18 Looking Back June 1996

It was a beautiful California morning, June 1, 1996. It was also two days before I was to be released from eleven years of burdensome imprisonment.

"Mr. Lacy, I need to see you in my office so you can sign some paperwork," Ms. K, my case manager said.

"I'll be right there Ms. K, give me a minute," I replied.

Ms. K was 5 feet four, blonde, green eyes and incredibly proportioned. You could tell from her shapely calves and legs that she worked out a lot; inmates called her Ms. K due to their inability to pronounce her last name.

"Are you sure these papers will get there in time, Ms. K?" I inquired.

"Sure, Mr. Lacy, it's only an itinerary of your travel time, the date and time you will arrive at the halfway house, so they will be expecting you. I'm sending it facsimile."

"Facsimile?" I looked confused.

"Yeah, fax," Ms. K answered with a smile.

I trusted she knew what she was doing.

"What are your release plans, Mr. Lacy? Eleven years is quite some time."

"I plan on becoming a youth counselor, Ms. K. I want to help young people get their priorities in order," I beamed with true emotion, convinced that I was qualified for that particular field.

"Well, I wish you luck Mr. Lacy. Please keep in mind that I went out of my way to get you six months halfway house. I think you need it considering the amount of time you spent incarcerated. Don't make me look bad," Ms. K said in a serious tone.

"Thanks Ms. K, but I'll be letting myself down more than anyone. Good looking out." I smiled.

"I won't be here tomorrow or the day after. Monday morning I'll walk you through the administration to R and D for release. Will someone be picking you up or do you plan on catching the bus?" she asked.

"My girlfriend and friend will be here to pick me up and drive me to the halfway house," I answered.

"Okay, good. You will have three hours to report to the halfway house in El Monte once you are released," Ms. K informed me, finalizing the terms of my itinerary.

"So, that wraps it up, Mr. Lacy. See you on Monday morning."

"Alright Ms. K, thanks."

The next two days seemed forever to pass. Time seemed to stop on me. I could not sleep well thinking of what to expect of the future.

But, I'd come out a survivor mentally and physically. Well almost. It's safe to say that every man leaves something behind, especially after long term confinement. No one remains the same. It is difficult for a convict to spend any amount of years away from family and loved ones without losing any sanity or social skills.

The prisoner loses all legal rights upon entering prison. Administrators and staff continually remind the prisoner of this through their derogatory, dehumanizing treatment of the prisoner. One out of ten staff members treat the prisoner with respect, dignity and compassion. Those staff members are a rare breed in the penal system. They are often frowned upon by other staff for dealing with prisoners as a person with an identity. It is also fair to mention that the term inmate and convict used in this reading are not synonymous and are not interchangeable. An inmate is a resident of any penal institution or mental facility. He or she readily conforms to any agenda the administration feeds its population, even if that agenda is counterproductive to mental maturity or personal growth.

The inmate is mindless, has no opinions of his own and does little in regards to change. He is usually not creative nor does he think independently. He is totally dependent on administrators setting agendas for him. You can find this inmate playing institution sports day in and day out, at a card table playing endless games, or watching television in a hypnotic state. This person will no doubt leave prison with the same mindset in which he entered. However, a convict is the exact opposite of the inmate. His rebelliousness tells you that he does not feel comfortable being out of an environment where he has no control.

He refuses to conform to codes that promote stagnation or humiliation. Most often he will opt out for segregation instead. The convict is self assured and confident of who he is, always on a course of self improvement. You will normally find this prisoner in the law library trying to liberate himself from his confines or partaking in college courses and other studies. During leisure hours he is reading or working out to keep his body and mind fine tuned. The convict is respectful of his peers and realizes that he is his own worst enemy. The very reason why he is so motivated to change.

Spending years at a time warehoused the convict battles stagnation at all cost. When the inmate is paroled he has unrealistic goals and dreams. He returns to a more modernized technologically advanced society in which he now after many years of dependency must try to survive. Perhaps it is due to social changes in society that causes the way its people feel about the incarcerated, those stigmas being formed through America's tough on crime propaganda. But, for whatever reasons, rehabilitation is a thing of the past, leaving the parolee bitter and maladjusted. When he is released to society you will often find he has no meaningful work or vocational skills.

Monday June 3, 1996

I stood at the cashier window and received fifty dollars in cash that was in my prison account.

"Good luck to you Mr. Lacy, hope I don't see you back in here," Ms. K said.

"Don't worry, you won't be seeing me again," I said with confidence.

A guard escorted me to the front gate of the prison. The warmth of the California sun beamed on my face. Realizing at this point my freedom was no dream, I walked a few steps, looked over my shoulder and flipped the bird at the guard as his face turned beet red.

"Adios amigo," I managed a shit-eating grin.

The guard who was habitually an asshole sneered, "Go home, Lacy."

"I'm just saying--," I uttered as the prison gate slammed in my face.

I disliked the keepers since I entered prison. My psychological profile penned me as someone who did not like authority. I never understood how a normal individual could apply for a job that only a moron would feel comfortable doing. I guess the same is said about people putting themselves in situations that result in incarceration. Whichever way, I was glad that I didn't have to deal with the insanity any longer.

I was greeted in the parking lot by my homie Preston, a burly ex-convict who had a passion for Dom Perignon.

229

"Give me one hot, one cold," he'd say when ordering the expensive champagne. We befriended one another during my stint in Terminal Island Prison where we were confined to the same housing unit. Preston's release came up a couple years before mine.

"Keep your head up, homie; I'll scoop you when your date comes."

"A'ight, playa," I replied.

Preston, having kept his promise, arranged to drive me to the Work Furlough Program (halfway house) in El Monte, California on the day of my release. Normally three to six months before an inmate's date prison administrators grant inmates an opportunity for early release provided the inmate maintained good conduct.

At the Work Furlough Program a parolee seeks employment during the day hours until employment is secured. After obtaining employment, the parolee is allowed weekend passes to spend time with family members. This facilitates the parolee's gradual return to society.

Preston's grin widened into a smile when he saw me. "Hey homie, welcome back. How you feel?" he asked extending his arms to embrace me.

"I'm good, homie. There is no better feeling than this."

I looked around breathing in the fresh air on the outside of the prison.

"Where is Michelle?" I asked, puzzled.

Michelle was my girlfriend. She was supposed to ride with Preston the morning of my release to pick me up.

"Michelle is in the car, homie."

As we reached the car, Michelle was getting out. I saw my woman dressed in a way I hadn't seen her before due to strict codes at prison visits. Michelle, a pecan-complected woman, wore a sexy hot pink mini dress with a v-cut exposing her cleavage. Her 44dd's were barely contained. She also sported pink pumps to match.

As our eyes met, her face lit up with joy. She rushed towards me, jumping off her feet and into my strong arms squeezing me tightly.

"I love you, daddy," she said smothering me with kisses, tears flowing from her eyes.

"Then why are you crying sweetness, if you love me?" I asked looking directly in her eyes.

"Because I am happy to see you. Plus I'm glad you are finally out of that place," she cried.

"Michelle, don't you worry everything will be okay now."

"Mmph! Mmph," Preston cleared his throat, trying not to sound like he was interrupting the private moment.

"Homie, you're due to the halfway house in four hours. Let's stop and get you something to grub on then I'll drop you and Michelle off at my place so the both of you can spend some time alone."

"Well let's shake this spot," I smiled.

"Right on homie."

"Where you want to eat, hon?" Michelle interjected.

"I think I have a taste for some jambalaya," I responded still thinking about the mention of privacy with Michelle.

"There is a take-out on Crenshaw Boulevard that makes the bomb jambalaya and it's on the way to my crib," Preston added.

"Let's roll," I said.

"Okay, jambalaya it is," Michelle squeaked.

"What an airhead," I smiled. But she has the most beautiful personality. A million dollar heart to match.

The Cadillac sung softly down the winding road away from the prison. The years I spent in federal prison were quite an experience.

I stared out the car window and realized how different society was from what I had imagined. I was absolutely taken aback viewing my surroundings. It seemed as if it were all a dream. I could not believe that I was finally out.

◆ ◆ ◆

The Cadillac pulled in front of M&M's, a popular eatery on Martin Luther King and Crenshaw Boulevard. M&M's burned some of the finest soul food dishes. The tire hit the curb shaking me out of my stupor. Apparently I had been day dreaming.

"Damn, that was some crazy shit."

"We're here hon," Michelle said reaching in her bra removing a roll of scrilla.

"That's it, lucky money," I smiled, stuffing the bills in my pocket.

"Be right back sexy," I said kissing her on the cheek.

"You want anything while I'm inside, Preston?"

"I'm straight, homie, good looking, though."

"How about you, baby?"

"Same as you, babe," Michelle answered.

"Oh! Get a pack of Newports," Michelle hollered through the window.

"Aight, babes!"

The cashier who worked the soul food joint eyed me up and down as I strolled through the door.

"Damn, that nigga is buff," she said under her breath.

I acquired a sculptured physique in prison, from years on top of years of methodical weight lifting and calisthenics. I had eighteen inch arms. I also sported washboard abs. The woman would bet a dollar to a donut that I had just gotten out of prison.

"Sir, may I take your order?"

The woman smiled sweetly, revealing pearly white teeth that highlighted her cocoa brown flawless complexion. Her long brunette hair rested past her shoulders.

"Yeah, I'd like to have the jambalaya dish please," I said returning the smile.

"Does a name go with your smile or are you going to leave me in a state of curiosity?" I asked. Damn, she is fine.

"Ha ha, you so silly," she laughed.

"My name is Yasmine, what's your's?"

"My name is Lacy, baby, and I don't see a damn thing funny around here. Not for reals, just kidding. Nice to meet you, Jasmine."

"It's Yasmine," she giggled.

"Oh, my bad, Yas-mine," I pronounced slowly, while thinking of something else clever to say.

"Yeah, that's it," she smiled.

"Can I ask you a question?" Yasmine whispered.

"Sure, go ahead and ask," I said moving closer toward the woman as if she held some sort of freaky secret.

"Have you been to the pen?" she nervously blurted out, appearing embarrassed by asking such a question.

"Yeah, as a matter of fact I have," I answered with no shame.

"But what gave you that indication?"

"It's the way you walk," Yasmine said.

"The way I walk?"

"Well, you walk like you are in a war zone," Yasmine laughed.

"Excuse me, I don't know if you are from around here, but this is South Central Los Angeles. Home of the Crips and Bloods. Where the L.A.P.D. shoot first and ask questions later. Need I say more?" I shot back.

"I'm no new booty. I'm a native Angeleno myself, born and raised in the city of Angels, so don't be so serious sweety. I was just kidding," the woman laughed.

"So is that good or bad?" I asked.

"Is what good or bad?" she sounded confused.

"That I've been to the pen," I answered.

"I'm not the one to judge any man. Plus my baby brother is in the pen. You'd think there is a war on black men in America the way they are locking brothers up in record numbers," she stated matter of factly.

"I hear you. You are politically correct," I added. "Well, here's your order and it was nice talking to you," she said smiling.

"The pleasure is mine, Nubian princess. By the way, I think you are gorgeous."

"Thank you," she blushed.

I shot my compliment, wondering if it would have any effect on overwhelming the woman's feminine nature.

"If at all possible, a young guy would love to conversate with you again. Do you mind?" I added.

The trap had been set. All she had to do was bite and I knew I could have her.

"I don't know if you are all that young," she capped back playfully, "but I don't mind kicking it with you again. You can reach me at 310-2864."

On my way back to the caddie, I was accosted by a homeless man who startled me. His hair was dried and matted, he also wore filthy clothes.

"Mr., do you have twenty-five cents?" the homeless man asked, revealing a rotted teeth smile.

Initially, I viewed the homeless man with contempt, disgust, and judgment; thinking what a shame. However, his humble demeanor caused me to re-evaluate my judgment about him.

"Sure man, why not," I answered, reaching into my pocket pulling out a dollar as the grin widened on his face.

Twelve years ago poverty had not been as widespread as it was today. Although there had been a problem with homelessness in the past, in recent years there had been an emergence of young people roaming the streets without home or shelter. Poverty had struck America's youth.

Opening the Caddie door, I was bombarded by a cloud of smoke.

"Mmph! Mmph! Damn homie, whatcha do, get lost in there?" Preston asked while choking on a blunt.

Blunts are marijuana rolled in cigar paper that is popular among marijuana smokers. The pair was listening to *"America's Nightmare"* by Spice One, a bay area rapper.

Lost in the euphoria, they hadn't noticed anything outside of the slick lyrics and bomb beats.

"Yeah, Foolio, I got lost alright. It looks as if the both of you are lost," I said, irritated about them smoking blunts.

It upset me because I was fresh out and already being subjected to violating my parole. If L.A.P.D. routinely stopped the vehicle and found marijuana, I would have been arrested and my parole automatically revoked. Ownership of the vehicle or who possessed the marijuana would have not mattered in my case.

◆ ◆ ◆

So the world moves on, I thought. While catching a view of society from within the confines of the Caddie, I saw two children racing their bikes while a small dog ran close behind barking at their feet. When you're young, you're innocent and haven't a care in the world, I smiled outwardly, while noticing the contrast of the world I now knew, compared to the hell I had just been released from.

The Fleetwood Cadillac finally rested at 42nd and Denker Avenue.

"Here are the keys to my crib, Lace; don't do anything I wouldn't do," Preston joked.

"Forget you fat boy!" Michelle snapped.

"Aight," I interrupted. "What time you bouncin' back through?"

The tires screeched, in front of the curb and the Cadillac jumped into action, leaving me without a reply. When the smoke cleared Michelle and

I were just stepping inside the small home.

"This is really nice," Michelle said in awe.

The area of 42nd and Denker Avenue is a high crime area, also gang infested. Yet, decent people still reside in homes around the Denker area, refusing to be overrun by the saturation of negative individuals bent on self destruction.

From outside of the small home Preston lived in, you could not tell the value that was put into it. Preston had been hitting the crap joints and good fortune was bestowed upon him. During his winning streaks he put money into the home, installing plush wall-to-wall carpet and a surround sound stereo system. There was a digital wall model television in the living room and the bathroom had been remodeled to fit a Jacuzzi style tub.

"This is off the hook," I said.

"Is this really Preston's home?" Michelle asked.

"Yep, his mom passed away a few years ago, leaving it to him."

"She obviously didn't leave it like this," I said amazed that a house in the ghetto could contrast so much with what was going on outside of it.

Sitting down on one of the fluffy comforters, we looked into each other's eyes romantically.

"Sweetheart, I'm excited about us finally being able to spend time together in privacy," I said, holding her hand softly.

"It's not really about sex, baby, but you and I being together without the keepers watching our every move," I whispered.

"Yeah, babes, I feel you. I waited so long for this day. Right now I'm going to have you," Michelle said sensually as she began disrobing, letting her mini-dress fall to the floor, exposing huge breast.

"Mmph!" I mumbled unable to control my nature, not really wanting to, "You have the body of a Nubian goddess," I said pleasingly.

Michelle smiled. She knew she was a breast man's dream. I grabbed Michelle and kissed her uncontrollably. She had been undressing me in the process. Falling back on the comforter, I entered her slowly as she moaned. We made love passionately and methodically.

Thinking about the numerous years I had gone without sex having to masturbate to relieve my sexual tensions, I surged with a tenacity of overwhelming lust. Our love moans intensified signaling that the sexual encounter had reached its peak. As the orgasms started to flow, our bodies jerked in rhythm. We were experiencing a state of bliss, convulsions gravitating from somewhere deep down. Then our bodies calmed as we slumped in each other's embrace breathing heavily.

"I love you," Michelle whispered in a sexy tone.

"I love you too sexy," I managed to speak through excited breathing.

"Do you really mean it, boo?" she asked while looking into my eyes.

"Michelle, listen and please understand," I whispered matching her gaze, "I don't know if you realize it or not, but you are the best thing that has happened to me. Our love is a true love, and I want to be there for you until the end of time."

"Baby you sure know how to say the right things," Michelle said, flushed.

I cemented the foundation of love and loyalty Michelle had for me. Although we had formed a bond since our meeting, sex had not come into play. Now that it had, the woman felt she had found true love.

While our love was still on the horizon we embraced and made love again...

"BAM! BAM! BAM! Open the door! This is the police," the man said in an obvious attempt to disguise his voice.

"Nice try asshole," I replied. "The police don't announce who they are any more, they just kick the door in."

"Ain't that right," Michelle laughed. "Come on in fool, we're dressed now."

"It's that time, homie," Preston said as he stepped through the door. "We got to get you to the halfway house on time."

"Give me a minute. I'm on my way now," I said, searching for my socks.

We headed down Denker Avenue, made a right turn on King Boulevard, and drove east towards Figueroa Street where we jumped on the Harbor Freeway destined for the suburb of El Monte.

Chapter 19 El Monte Halfway House

We listened to the song by Miche'le "*Something in my heart*" as the Cadillac flowed comfortably through freeway traffic. Like a Vietnam Vet having flashbacks, my mind wandered through the past sorting out nightmarish events I'd experienced as a convict caged like an animal in the federal system.

It's like another planet in there I thought, reflecting on the cold chill environment. The years in solitary, sadistic guards, and angry faces. I gradually grew into a sense of hopelessness each calendar year, with no outlook for the future.

I remembered the senseless violence and aggression I had experienced on many occasions being baited from time to time into foolishness; the frustrations of prison life causing me to spin out of control. I was free now and could put those experiences behind me.

The El Monte Halfway House was the last stop before I parted with my girlfriend Michelle, and homie Preston. It was a thirty minute drive on the 10 freeway from South Central, Los Angeles, more or less depending on the traffic. The surrounding neighborhood is comprised of working class whites and Latinos; the area is fairly clean and quiet.

Halfway houses are located in undesirable high crime areas that are saturated with drugs and prostitution. El Monte was one of the exceptions.

"We're here homie. Not a bad looking joint," Preston remarked.

"Give me a kiss daddy, I'm gonna miss you so call me tonight after you get settled in, kay?" Michelle said teary eyed.

"You're such a cry baby. Come here, give me some of that sweetness," I said cheering her up.

"I'm calling you as soon as you get home. It ain't no limits as how long we can talk anymore either," I smiled.

"Okay," she beamed.

"Holla at you in a minute Preston. Scoop up Michelle for me and bring her to see me tomorrow playa."

"Fo shizy, homie."

The Cadillac screeched out of the parking lot as I made my way up to the halfway house to report in.

"Hello!" I smiled at the receptionist.

"I just paroled this morning. I'm supposed to be checking in today."

"Please have a seat Mr. Lacy. We have been expecting you. You're an hour late."

"My bad. The afternoon traffic was extremely heavy," I lied.

"Yeah sure. Nine out of ten of you parolees come straggling in late on you first day out the pen," she snapped.

"Do you mind introducing yourself to me? I'd at least like to know someone before they call me a liar," I said in a smug tone.

"Never mind my name, be seated and fill out these forms please. The program director will speak with you shortly," she said paying me no mind.

Some people are just mean and ornery for no reason, I thought as I snatched the papers out of her hand.

The program director conducted an intake screening, asking me frivolous questions and giving information that was common knowledge. He also orientated me on halfway house policies and procedures which seemed to take hours. I could hardly wait until I had a chance to go lay down and think, my mind was already reeling from being free. Yet, it was that exhilarating feeling the enabled me to sit through the boring details of the intake.

"Yes!" I smiled inside.

As the director carried on his orientation, all I was thinking was that I finally made it. I waited so long to be outside those walls. I thought about Michelle and our lovemaking only hours ago. The passionate sex had brought us full circle. The loneliness over the years had miraculously faded.

The things I experienced over the next six months seemed magnified. Everyday things people take for granted, a parolee takes notice of.

For example, in prison, you will not see children. Unless you are fortunate enough for your family members to visit you on a regular basis. You will not experience the opportunity to watch them grow, hear them laugh, cry, or watch them play. Adults grow weary of children quickly due to the fact they are rarely absent of them, thus they are not missed as much.

I experienced many other things that prison erases from memory over time; driving a car, walking in the park, eating fast food in a restaurant, shopping at the mall, being outside after dark. Simple things people do daily, yet don't appreciate.

Most convicts when released have no one whom they can count on in terms of assistance and guidance through a complex society. A lot of them have burned bridges in the past with family or friends who have turned their back on the parolee, leaving him to fend for himself.

If you make it a practice to be good and real to others, no matter what your circumstances or troubles, you will always find someone with an open heart who will remember and acknowledge your true qualities as a man.

My support consisted of a tight woven circle of compassionate women. First and foremost, my Mother who would bend over backwards to assist me in getting back on track. Then there was Michelle who made sure that all necessities were handled at home, leaving us worry free from the basics.

Krystle, my teenage friend, was always there from day one, pulling strings when needed. Sheila, my childhood sweetheart, kept in touch from time to time and was a constant reminder of my past. She knew me better than anyone and urged me to do right for once.

"You have made those jails out of house and home, man. Do yourself some good and enjoy what life you have left. I love you like you are my brother. We have been through thick and thin," Sheila said keeping it real.

Edwina, Jennifer, and Dana also showered me with unwavering support.

"I know you're not working yet so I mailed you a money order for you to use as you please," Edwina said.

"Sis, you didn't have to do that, I'm straight," I responded.

"Boy, I'm not worried about what you're saying; if you need anything call me."

"Okay, sis," I answered shyly.

It's weird, but it's true. A real man will not continue to accept anything of value from sources that he loves and not give back without feeling like a "piece of work". A man will prefer to get his own, because only a man will do what a man has to do to take care of himself and not at the expense of others. Only the "pimp mentality" would allow a man to take advantage of his love ones because he can.

Outside living was good. So was the food. Meals in prison are the same week after week. If it's Monday, you know it's hamburger day; a small rotten piece of steer, most inmates opt not to consume.

There were also a lot of mental complexities that exist being confined. Being free from those set conditions is the ultimate feeling. But then guess what? You adopt another set of complexities in society.

Not being married brought about a situation where women were an issue. Although I was committed to Michelle, I was being pulled at on all sides. During the nineties, women adopted a new attitude about relationships with men and meeting them. The nineties woman was not hesitant on approaching men, initiating conversation and then ultimately asking the man on a future date, insisting on paying for it. I wasn't used to this. Some believe this somewhat turn around is due to available black men falling victim to imprisonment in record numbers. The ratio on the dating field being imbalanced, causing the single black female to be alienated and most often lonely.

As I stepped on the city bus wearing my new threads, I looked and felt like new money. Paying no special attention to the sea of faces, I sat in a seat near the driver not knowing someone had been watching my every move.

"Oh, you not gonna speak, huh?" the shrill voice raised slightly penetrating my ear canals.

Curious, I looked up and noticed the woman's eyes planted all over my face.

"Yeah, I'm talking to you," she said peering through the mirror located right above the driver's seat.

"Oh, my bad," I said smoothly, yet feeling a little intimidated about her assertiveness.

"I didn't even realize you spoke to me, sista," I said sheepishly to the female bus driver.

"How you doing anyway?" I blushed, unable to shift the situation and take over.

"I'm just saying, you are dressed real fly and I think you look good wearing those suspenders, too," she said making me feel like I was on Front Street.

"Oh yeah, thanks," I barely got out as I shifted around in my seat nervously.

"Could you please tell me when we reach Century Boulevard?" I asked.

"Sure. As a matter of fact it's a couple lights down," she answered.

"Thanks."

As the bus pulled away from the curb, I stood there damn near in disbelief.

Damn fool. I thought. You really blew that one. If she was a snake she would have bit you.

It was an experience in which taught me to recognize the game of seduction. Within the next several months, the euphoria of easy living started wearing thin when the reality of putting my goals into action surfaced and being laid back became a thing of the past.

Life is sweet when you first get out of prison; then you gradually awaken to life's reality and what needs to be done in order for survival.

If you don't have an agenda, you will always have one foot inside the penitentiary. Any miscalculation of ideas could send you back into the environment from which you came.

My short term and long term goals had no back doors. For someone who had been incarcerated eleven years my vision was not clear. I had no alternate plans in the event I could not reach my desired ones.

The dream of becoming a youth counselor ran into dead ends. In the state of California, most agencies require that you have a bachelors or masters degree and no criminal convictions of violence. Door after door of opportunity was shut in my face because of this.

The work furlough counselor recommended I put in applications for construction work.

"A lot of agencies will hire regardless of your criminal background. Most firms are just looking for able bodies who can do the labor and work," Jackie said.

Jackie was the halfway house employment coordinator. She assisted us with referrals and leads for jobs that parolees could work despite their criminal record. Federal parolees were covered by the Federal Bonding Program.

Taking her advice, I landed employment with a temporary agency that loaned workers to various work sites for average pay. For example, if company X paid the temporary agency twenty dollars per hour for a carpenter or laborer, the temporary agency would pay the temp worker ten dollars per hour and keep the difference for the cost of locating jobs for the worker.

My first job was with Border's Bookstores, contracting out as a carpenter. I was paid twelve dollars per hour. I telephoned Michelle at her job with the news.

"Babes, guess what?" I spoke into the phone proudly. "Yeah, sweetheart, what?" she answered.

"I got a job working construction. I start in the morning, five a.m."

"I'm happy for my man, now he can help provide for the two of us," her voice smiled over the phone.

"The two of who!" I asked raising my voice slightly.

"Your child and I; I'm pregnant," Michelle said.

"On the for reals?" I smiled.

"Are you black?" she joked. "I'll talk to you when you get in tonight."

"Bye."

"Bye, sweetness."

"God has surely blessed me right now," I thought.

For the next few months I worked at various construction locations: J.P. Getty Center, K-Marts and CBS studio where I had the opportunity to personally meet the stunning and beautiful former Price is Right model and actress, Kathleen Bradley. She is also known for her role played as the character Mrs. Parker in the movie "Friday".

After work hours Michelle and I played name games for our future child.

"If it's a girl, I want to name her Diamone Michelle Lacy," she said.

"It's gonna be a boy, so no need to worry about that," I smiled.

"Then what will we name him?" Michelle asked.

"I dunno," I answered, dumbfounded that I had not thought of it yet.

"So, now that I'm pregnant when are we getting married, my future husband?" she asked.

"Married? Where is all this coming from?" I asked.

"You promised me that we'd get married when you got out. Don't have amnesia, Mr. Lacy."

"I said that?" I answered wearing a shit-eating grin.

"Yeah, okay, right," she pouted.

"Aight babe, I remember now, I was just teasing, damn!" I played. "Since I'm working how about we set a date of January next year?" I said now serious.

"Quit playing, Lacy," Michelle said.

"Okay, okay next month, babe," I lied just to get around the subject.

"You think you're slick, nigga. I'm holding you to that though."

"Whatever!" I said, exposing my true feelings about getting married.

"Yeah, that's right," Michelle said unable to control her composure.

"Go ahead, show your true colors," she added.

"Damn baby, chill out," I said wanting to avoid an argument.

"Naw, man. I knew when you got out it would come to this. It's exactly what I expected. But it was me who visited you every weekend. It was me who kept money on your books. You don't have to lie to kick it," she screamed angrily, clearly in her feelings.

"Baby, you are straight trippin, nutting up on me for no reason at all, acting out of your element. Our wedding rings that are on layaway at the mall doesn't mean anything I guess either. Oh! My bad. It's supposed to be a surprise, but I guess I'm lying about that too! I've sacrificed a portion of my paycheck every week to pay for those rings, since you want to throw things up in my face. I see now you don't take anything I say serious," I performed.

The ploy was unrehearsed, but I acted it well. I decided to go there when I saw reason could not overrule emotion. Women are very sensitive and emotional beings. A man doesn't stand a chance when a woman feeds on her innermost emotions. Clashing head-on only makes matters worse.

Simple psychology softens the heart and allows room to plan your next move. Like an actress wearing stage makeup, Michelle flipped the script and started crying tears of joy.

"Oh baby, you got our wedding rings? I'm sorry babes!" Michelle said, kissing me affectionately all over my face.

"Naw, don't be sorry now," I played, smiling inside.

"I'm thinking about taking them off layaway since you say I'm lying to kick it," I added rubbing it in.

"Nice outburst, Michelle," I thought, knowing I would have more time to dodge the wedding I regretted planning during one of our prison visits.

Chapter 20 The Last Dance

People can sometimes dictate what their future will be like and then other times events happen when we least expect them. It's how effectively you deal with these situations that determine their outcome. It happened one night while I was on a break at CBS studio. I called my Mom from work as I normally did and she delivered the news.

"Michelle is in Daniel Freeman Hospital, son. You need to go over there to see her when you get off work."

"What's going on, what happened, Mom?" I asked, my heart racing.

"Michelle had a miscarriage sometime today."

"You alright, son?" she asked.

"Yeah Mom, I'm okay. I'm leaving work early to give her some emotional support at the hospital."

Michelle took the miscarriage hard, becoming very emotional thereafter. I can't really say if it was because she knew I was so anxious to experience the birth of our first child, or that the psychology of experiencing a miscarriage was too much for her mentally and physically.

However, it left a mark on our relationship that would chip away each day at the foundation we built over time. Not understanding

Michelle's need to recover mentally on her own clock frustrated me even more. I pressured Michelle to pay more attention to romance.

This caused her to pull even further away, seeing me as callous and uncaring. Our relationship nose-dived in a matter of weeks. We barely got along anymore. Communicating turned into shouting matches. The desire for sex and romance became a thing of the past. I cannot vividly describe the feelings I harbored, the confusion and alienation I felt.

Being locked away in a hostile prison environment year after year did not equip me with the ability to be able to cope with situations as such. It was totally alien to me.

Sometimes women need space so that they can get into their own heads emotionally and deal with whatever's going on with them. Men, you need to give your woman space or you may jeopardize your relationship. A woman does not want to be with a man who is uncaring or insensitive to her emotional needs.

To make matters worse, the contracts I had been working slowed down to a halt due to money issues between the contractors and the temporary agency. Another devastating event occurred. Sheila, my teenage sweetheart and friend, passed away in her sleep. The coroner ruled it as heart failure. Sheila was only thirty-six years old. She left behind two young boys.

Too many setbacks were happening at once. I started drinking which resulted in a relapse, reeling me further into the abyss of self destruction.

Every effort to come out of this despair was thwarted by me using cocaine. I neglected my capabilities to be patient, and allow the hardships to naturally work themselves out.

Our relationship hit a dead end and we separated. The end of the relationship seemed to be the tranquil I needed. Since my release from prison, Michelle had totally enveloped me. We consumed each other day in and day out.

In order to become a part of society again and experience any long term success, the parolee must establish patience, never giving up hope of achieving his goals.

Goals must be set, starting with short terms first. In some cases, the parolee will find he has to endure bumps in the road until he starts seeing any real progress. Catching up with the rest of society does not happen overnight. When the parolee understands this he is then able to make greater gains in cementing the path towards remaining free in the outside world.

One step backward could land a parolee in prison for a period of time or perhaps the rest of his life. He has to continually adjust and think clearly to remain focused. Failure to adjust may bring about measures that are desperate and desperate measures causes desperate actions.

The Caddie pulled up behind me. HONK! HONK!

"What's up, homie?" the man in the Caddie shouted. Recognizing the face, I immediately responded.

"Man, I ain't seen you in months," I cheesed.

"Where you headed?" he asked.

"I'm on my way to the G.R. building," I answered.

"The bus should be here shortly," I said without shame.

"Get in homie. I'll give you a ride."

"Cool! These buses ain't nuthin nice," I grinned.

"I feel you, homie. I wish I could have run into you some months earlier. Me and some homies hit a nice lick, but homie I'm broke already."

"I'm feeling you," I responded. "How did you break yourself so fast, homie?" I inquired.

"You know how it is taking care of a family. Plus, I have a bit of a gambling problem."

"Oh, I see."

"Listen, homie. I need to run something by you," he whispered as if someone else were around.

"I have a lick set for a meal ticket," he said.

I listened eagerly and my hands started to sweat as they always do at the mention of getting money in a major way.

"One of my homies is backing out, that scary ass nigga," he went on.

"My nigga, I need someone with experience to go in with me. I'm telling you off the top, there will be a third person if you decide to go," he said studying my face closer.

"Are you game?"

I thought about the General Relief check I was about to pick up and knew it was a joke. My greed overrode common sense. I thought about the amount of money involved and knew I could fix everything with that kind of cash. Life would be so much easier, I foolishly thought.

"What kind of lick is this and where," I asked.

"We ain't gotta do a lot of rapping about who, what and when. If you are down I'll fill you in on all you need to know later," he said impatiently.

"Hold it right here homie, you passed my stop," I said looking out the rearview.

"Hit me on my hip later," I said pointing to my beeper.

"I'm with you," I said stepping out the Caddie.

As I left the General Relief Building my mind was in a daze. Partly from the thought of getting major money, and also from the numerous papers I had to fill out the entire day to get the measly two hundred and twelve dollars and food stamps that were suppose to carry me to the next month.

My mind was exhausted thinking about the upcoming heist. I calculated the risks involved carefully. I could be a millionaire overnight or spend a very long term in prison.

On a balancing scale any level-headed individual would have had nothing to consider. No amount of money is worth risking your life, or imprisonment, for any amount of years. I still had a lot to learn.

1 April 1997 9:30a.m.

It was a sunny California morning and the million dollar heist had already gone sour. Having already loaded the Ford Bronco with a substantial amount of cash, the female bandit drove away from the north side exit down Artesia Boulevard.

Within two blocks she would near the oncoming ramp that would put the utility vehicle, the cash, her life, on the freeway and out of harm's reach. Turning on the handheld police scanner that she carried to affect her safe return, she listened closely as police radio dispatchers communicated with patrol and helicopter units as they combed the surrounding area of the bank.

"All units to the strip mall on Hawthorne Boulevard. Possible robbery suspects in the area, over and out," the dispatcher announced.

"10/4," a respondent answered.

The female bandit, now miles away, lit a Newport cigarette and inhaled deeply. She listened to the situation that was going on back at the bank, praying that her confederates would escape the dragnet.

As she thought about the cash she was sitting on, a moment of guilt and shame overcame her. But no sooner than it did she smiled because she knew in her heart they would all make it back home.

Patrick Brown pulled his van towards the curb and flagged down one of the prowling units.

"Hey, officer, I saw two black males come out of the bank removing latex gloves and ski masks. They walked over that way toward the strip mall," he said pointing across the street.

The two bandits walked into the clothing store unnoticed.

"Say homie, we gotta split here, we don't need to be together. If one of us gets cracked he looks out for the other," one of the bandits said.

"That's a bet. I'm laying low here," the other bandit replied, giving his man daps as he walked back out.

The morning sun glimmered, causing the bandit to squint slightly. As he focused his eyes he noticed there was not a soul in sight. At the same time he heard familiar words.

"Police! Get down!"

He found himself on the pavement wondering how his body responded so quickly. He was laying face down, popping sounds ricocheting all around him. The shots were not clear, though. They seemed distant, as if he were hearing them from afar. He never knew it but a bullet tore through the top of his head. He saw the pool of blood gushing out on the sidewalk into the gutter. He tried to move but he couldn't feel himself. There was so much pain he could not think clearly. Then suddenly he died. His lifeless form lay there as the SWAT team kicked his body violently.

"Get your hands behind your back asshole!" the crazed policeman shouted, not knowing the man was already dead.

Inside the clothing store the other bandit bunkered in. Hearing shots, he immediately went into hiding, knowing it would be fruitless to engage in a firefight. The SWAT team ordered everyone out of the strip mall by bullhorn until it was completely empty. They entered each store premises carrying M-16 assault rifles and wearing body armor. Three hours later they left the building with a suspect in tow. It was Kaos the K-9 that signaled the suspects presence as he attacked.

Driving the last mile to safety, the female heard the frightening and unexpected over the police scanner.

"We have one suspect down and a possible suspect in custody. We're bringing him in," the SWAT team leader radioed to dispatch.

The woman screamed, "I HATE YOU! I HATE YOU! I HATE YOU FUCKIN BASTARDS!!"

She wept uncontrollably, knowing the fate of her confederates. Pulling out of sight, she collapsed her head in her hands and cried.

At the station the police interrogated the bloodied and exhausted suspect who refused to answer any questions. "What's your name?"

"What were you doing in that store?"

"Who is the asshole we took down?"

"Where is the other bandit?"

"Where is the money?" the detectives badgered without a response.

"You're going down for a long time. Do yourself some good and tell us where the other bandit is hiding," the detectives continued to pester.

"His prints will be back shortly. We'll know who he is then," the homicide detective said.

"Until then, let's get down to the crime scene and see if we can get some statements from witnesses."

I sat in the cold cell in a zombie-like state, devastated from the deadly set of events. I thought about the future of my life, knowing it would be bleak.

Three federal marshals walked into the substation carrying a briefcase with documents and restraints. They were going to transfer the prisoner the local authorities had been holding over to federal custody.

"We are in receipt of your fax and got here as soon as we could. We are here to pick up one of ours," Agent Brenner said to the desk sergeant.

"No problem, sir; we were expecting you. The prisoner is in the bullpen, come with me please," Sergeant Jackson responded, clamping down on the unlit cigar between his teeth.

The marshals surrounded the holding tank as Sergeant Jackson ordered the jailer to open the door.

"Smitty, open tank #5. We need a prisoner in here."

I awoke from my fitful daze and it pained me to look up.

The federal agent spoke in a baritone voice, one of authority, "James Lacy Jr., is that your true name?"

"Yes, it is."

"We are here to take you into federal custody, to take you to the Metropolitan Detention Center downtown. You are charged with 2114, Title 18 U.S.C. Armed Bank Robbery. You have the right to remain silent and anything you say can and will be used against you in a court of law..."

The words fell on deaf ears. As the agents read me my Miranda rights I stared straight through them. My eyes had that far away look. All I could think of was what a lame I had been, duping myself into believing we could pull it off. Sometimes external factors take control of our internal thoughts, clouding one's judgment causing foolish actions. If only I could turn back the clock giving myself another opportunity to choose wisely.

Overcoming challenges are sometimes painful. By maintaining a positive outlook any individual can move past these challenges without falling flat on his face. I thought about my nieces, nephews, sisters and Mom. How during one time or another I had been away from them, missing out on that family bond. What could I say to them now?

The federal marshals van rolled smoothly and quietly through the city streets. The window was tinted so you could barely see that I was sitting in the back seat with twenty pounds of leg and waist chains. As I looked out the tinted window I studied the faces moving about. They looked tranquil and serene. In another world it seemed; a world in which I could find no place.

The van rolled to a stop at an intersection. A woman with a small child sat at a bus stop. She squinted her eyes trying to peer through the van's tinted glass windows, curious about the occupants. She saw a shadowy figure staring back at her. She never saw the tears that continuously streamed from my eyes.

Life is precious and you only live once; may as well make good of each day that you are blessed with. The life of crime and glamour in the streets is not as rewarding as it seems...

Epilogue

Statistics indicate that the first year of parole is the most critical period for the parolee. It is the period where the highest rate of recidivism occurs. I, too, became part of this statistic by putting myself at risk inside of a year. There are over two million men and women incarcerated, on parole or probation in the United States. A large percent of this number are our nation's youth. Many of them would not be in their predicament if they had received proper guidance, education and mentoring in their formative years. Another reason for the growing incarceration rate is the drugs which have saturated our communities. We need to act now to stop this cycle that has destroyed the family structure and values.

More emphasis should be geared toward cultivation and educating the mindset of youth. Society spends more money on incarceration than on education. Prison is the most dehumanizing situation a person can experience; it stunts one's potential for growth. Rehabilitation is only effective where true rehabilitation exists. Not likely in a prison setting.

The family unit must take responsibility in uplifting one another and practicing the basic fundamentals of life: Honesty, self-respect, responsibility, determination and unity. Remember the youth of today may be our leaders of tomorrow.

Peace

About the Author

James Lacy was raised in South Central, Los Angeles.

He was eventually sent to prison and while doing time educated himself. The Author became interested in writing, and his first book, *Hope Beyond Measure*, is both a product of his life on the streets of South Central and his desire to become a writer.

Lacy has also dedicated his life to working with at-risk youth, and dreams of one day developing a mentoring program that will place them in contact with positive aspects of their lives.

You may email James at: jlacy2014@yahoo.com .

www.ingramcontent.com/pod-product-compliance
Lightning Source LLC
Chambersburg PA
CBHW070314260626
47160CB00003B/835